Academy

Assassination

Hannah Jones

Academy Assassination

Academy

Assassination

Academy Assassination

ISBN: 978-1-3999-7821-7

1st Edition [2024]

Meet the Characters

Miss Frances Garnham ~ 24 ~ Frances is friendly, outgoing and creative. She is curious, stubborn and always follows her gut instincts.

Detective Chief Inspector Barry Hughes ~ 52 ~ Barry is very old-fashioned, blunt and likes to get jobs done as quickly as possible.

Detective Inspector Jonathan Birch ~ 28 ~ Jonathan is very kind to all those he meets and is willing to try new ways of investigating but doesn't want to go against the boss.

Adeline Stevenson ~ 45 ~ Adeline is welcoming to all those in her school, she can be quite talkative and can waffle on, she has been known to let things slip.

Alice McKenzie ~ 23 ~ Alice is very kind-hearted, friendly to everyone, but can be timid, anxious, overthinks and doesn't want to upset anyone.

Caroline Macintosh ~ 57 ~ Caroline is polite but has very old-fashioned views, believes that her view is correct and that she knows best. She is very opinionated, blunt and can be brutal.

Max Henderson ~ 34 ~ Max is bubbly, energetic and can have a laugh, but can be serious when the time comes. Max is friendly and approachable to all, but he can be very hidden and vague about things at times.

Ian Marshall ~ 49 ~ Ian is quite closed and very posh. He is very serious and knowledgeable which means he tends to peer down his nose at the younger and less experienced teachers.

Agatha Davidson ~ 36~ Agatha is very jolly, chatty, welcoming, friendly and humorous. She is quite casual in both life and in teaching, she doesn't like there being any conflict. Agatha is open and can be known to say things without thinking.

Grant Kennedy ~ 35 ~ Grant is average, polite and quite quiet, keeping themselves to themselves. He doesn't like to get involved in the drama and just wants to get on with his job. Grant is a silent watcher and because he is not very talkative can be seen as quite awkward.

Charlotte Thompson ~ 29 ~ Charlotte is academically minded, if they are not teaching or marking, they are likely to have their head in a book. Socialising is not her thing. She is very well spoken and always has an academic and logical answer on hand.

Grace Taylor ~ 60 ~ Grace has vast experiences from a well lived life, she really enjoys her job and is always on hand to provide other staff members with a well needed boost. She is very kind, welcoming and loves the simple things in life.

Dylan Walker ~ 26 ~ Dylan is enthusiastic and throws himself into everything. He is quite humorous, very friendly and is someone everyone gets on with.

Harper Craig-Lawson ~ 22 ~ Harper is very kind, welcoming and friendly to all. She is very knowledgeable, hardworking and can be quite headstrong.

Amanda Morrison ~ 40 ~ Amanda is known for being the school gossip, she has all the latest news and is happy to share it with anyone who asks for it. She is friendly and approachable, although this can change depending on who she is talking to and is normally found filing her nails or gaining more gossip from parents.

Lennox and Mildred Campbell ~ 54 and 49 ~ Lennox and Mildred might have been married for years but they are still hopelessly in love. They are friendly with everyone and get on well with the children, Lennox likes to have a laugh with them whilst Mildred acts like a caring grandma and is often seen bringing in baked goods for the staff.

Kathleen Packer ~ 5 ~ Kathleen is polite and hardworking; however, she can be quite chatty. She notices things and will point out when things have changed and whether she likes it or not.

For my unhinged Bracket and my Bertie Boo, and
the rest of my family and friends x

Bardy-Doo 1954-2023 (Love you Dad, sorry you
never got to read this) x

Argumentative Arrival…

The quaint village of Bertley could only be described as an ideal countryside postcard. Surrounded by rolling farming fields and fresh vibrant green trees.

'Christ! How hard can it be to find a school in this village?' Exclaimed the driver of the sleek metallic *Fiesta* which trundled down the silent country roads.

Bertley is a village made up of winding country roads, with an array of detached and semi-detached houses dotted along either side. Some of the houses clearly being new builds with their symmetrical windows and immaculate structure, whilst others were much older houses; their golden bricks etched with decades of history. The old church is on the outskirts of the village. Frances knows this because she drove straight through the village whilst looking for the school. The church could only be what one might call a typical village church, the tall square steeple and stain glass windows gave Frances the sanctitude she needed to turn the car around and travel back into the village on her quest to find the school.

'Well all I need now is to find *Miss Marple* and I really will be in *St Mary Mead*,' Frances grumbled as she crawled back through the village. Instead, Frances did find the pub, it was only by chance as all the buildings seemed to blend into one. The only difference being a sign outside with the pub name and a slightly larger driveway which could hold four cars. At a closer look at the bar sign, the pub was known as *The Lost Cause* and had the image of two travellers looking perplexed on the edge of a field. Frances thought the pub would be more relatable if the sign was of her in her car looking for the school.

After what seemed like hours of searching, Frances finally came across a green school sign erected on a brick wall in a lay-by beside the main road. Her first perception of the school was that it looked like a large house behind a wooden gate.

'There must be additional buildings behind this... please say there are more buildings,' Frances begged; she hated tiny schools. Luckily for Frances the school was bigger than it seemed. The school is an oblong shape with a large hall at one end with some classes branching from it, with a long corridor leading to other classes, the staffroom and a school library. As the school gates leading to the car park were open, Frances put her car back into drive and slowly drove into the first free space she could find.

'Well, at least they were expecting me, I guess,' Frances sighed as she turned off the engine and collected her belongings. Her auburn hair fell past her shoulders as she stumbled out of the car. Something about the school made her feel funny like something wasn't right; and she didn't think it was just the size of the school.

As the car locked with a click and a flash of the headlights, Frances caught sight of the outfit she had pulled out of the wardrobe that morning. She wanted to be comfortable however she thought this was going too far, a hoodie and leggings paired with trainers did scream comfort but didn't correspond as well in a school environment.

Upon entering the reception area, Frances was met with a small tidy room made up of a couple of chairs for anyone waiting to be seen, a small reception desk and a printer hidden away in the corner. In the silence, she could hear a constant tapping of computer keys from the behind the glass window of the reception desk. On approaching the desk, she saw a stone-faced looking woman typing angrily into the computer. The look of the receptionist could only be characterised as... interesting. Her brunette hair, which was decorated with patchy blonde highlights, covered her unreadable face but that was mainly because her eyes were concealed underneath thick false eyelashes, but what really looked like wire brushes. Frances could now see the cause of the loud tapping which was created by the long acrylic claws on the end of the receptionist's fingers.

At this moment in time, Frances realised she must have zoned out trying to find the right words to sum up the person in front of her because the stone-faced woman was currently staring back at her with a dubious look on her face.

'Oh! Um... Hi... sorry,' Frances stuttered as she felt her face colour. 'Er... I'm Frances Garnham, the new year one teaching assistant?'

It felt like an age to Frances, but the receptionist's expression turned as her eyebrows raised and a smile grew on her face. 'Oh yeah! Hiya sweetie, how are ya? Yeah, we have been expecting you. Why don't you take a seat honey, and I will let the head know you are here. I'm Amanda by the way, the receptionist... obviously.' The receptionist cackled as she gestured to her surroundings. Frances laughed and pushed her metal rimmed glasses up her nose and headed towards one of the waiting chairs.

Sometime later a door creaked open.

'Good morning, you must be our new assistant?' Said a voice.

Frances stood up quickly and turned with her hand extended to face the voice. 'Yes, good morning. I'm Frances Garnham.'

The two shook hands and the voice gestured for Frances to follow her into the office. The office was small but inviting. There was a large desk with a black leather office chair and comfortable cushioned seats to the side of the door for any visitors to sit on. There were several quotes on the wall, supposedly meant to be inspirational but they didn't seem that way to Frances. One of the quotes was: *Together we stand, divided we fall.* Frances thought that really implied: *Follow our ways or good luck, you're on your own.* Above the desk Frances saw the quote: *Children are the future.* She had to stop herself from becoming *Whitney Houston* and singing at the top of her lungs. Instead, she took the seat offered to her and stayed quiet.

'Well Miss Garnham,' the woman cooed excitedly at Frances. 'May I start by saying welcome to Arrows Primary Academy. I am Adeline Stevenson, headteacher of the school.'

'Thank you and please call me Frances, I am still trying to get my head around being referred to by something other than my name as it were.' Both women laughed as Adeline reached across the desk to gather some forms for Frances to sign. Adeline was a petite woman-well petite to Frances anyway who was five foot seven-with slightly greying hair so she must have been in her mid-forties; not that the woman seemed to dress for her age as Adeline was currently styling a vibrant, multicoloured kaftan.

'I just need these forms filling out Frances, standard procedure you know how it is. I would have liked to have emailed them to you, but I don't get on well with technology you see,' Adeline chuckled as she meaninglessly shuffled the papers in her hands.

'No problem at all Mrs Stevenson, I can quickly fill them in now. Would it be possible to borrow a pen?' Frances reassured Adeline as she reached across for the papers.

'Adeline please,' she handed Frances the papers and a pen. 'Lovely, well once all that is done and dusted, I will take you on a tour and you can meet some of the staff!'

The tour of the school ended in the staffroom. The staffroom is cosy with lots of soft chairs and small sofas surrounding a small coffee table. There is a miniature confined kitchen area with the simple necessary facilities in the corner of the room.

'Right Frances, how about a quick cup of tea before I take you to meet the year one staff?' Adeline cheerfully called from inside the mug cupboard in the kitchen area.

'That sounds lovely,' Frances smiled as she settled herself into one of the comfy chairs.

By the time they had finished their drinks Frances and Adeline had gotten to know each other very well. Frances was just about to ask how Adeline got into teaching when suddenly a figure appeared in the doorway. The figure was male who had rugged brunette hair, a hint of stubble, dressed in a casual and slightly messy outfit.

'Ah perfect timing! Here's one of my staff members. Frances this is Max our year two teacher,' Adeline introduced gesturing towards the man.

'Nice to meet you, Frances. Welcome to Arrows,' Max greeted Frances. Up close she noticed a small gleam in his green eyes, and the fact that not only was he tall but from the grip of his handshake he was also well built.

'Hello, thank you. From what I have seen so far, it's a lovely school,' Frances responded kindly.

'Frances is our new year one teaching assistant,' Adeline added a slight thrill in her voice. It was at hearing this information that Max's face changed. The gleam in his eyes disappeared and the once smiling face turned to one of dread. It was just by chance that Frances heard Max's response.

'Well in that case, should I say good luck,' he scoffed giving Frances a look which said: *get out while you still can*, before excusing himself and leaving.

Frances' uncertainty increased; it seemed odd to her that a member of staff would show that much resentment towards another colleague in front of a new co-worker; especially on her first day.

'What am I getting myself into?' She thought.

Adeline sensing the distain in Max's reaction and the confusion showing on Frances' face tried to recover and put Frances at ease, although not as well as she would have liked. 'Oh, don't worry about that, some of the teachers always seem to be bickering it's nothing really,' Adeline chuckled as she waved her hand dismissively.

Frances nodded. 'I understand, it's bound to happen in the workplace from time to time.'

'Exactly! Oh, I am so glad you are here Frances,' Adeline shrieked. 'You will fit in so well here. You do find there are quarrels here and there. We are a real bunch of characters here… not that that's a bad thing you see, we all just have different personalities,' she quickly added.

'I am sure they are all lovely Adeline really,' Frances reassured her.

'Goodness me, what am I saying, scaring you off on your first day,' Adeline thought out loud, finishing with a slightly forced cackle.

Frances, sensing she needed to get out of here before Adeline had the opportunity to say anything else, she excused herself to go and get settled into her new classroom. Adeline seemed relieved of the escape route being given to her, breathing a sigh of relief as she gave Frances her parting words.

'Of course, dear, I am sure you could be spending your time more wisely instead of listening to me witter on. Well, if you feel you do need to get away from it all at any time, my office door is always open.'

The anxious feeling that was already in Frances' stomach tightened and her mind started to race with panicked thoughts:

What a weird thing to say…

What was so bad about working here? Working in year one?

What the hell was Frances getting herself into?

The classroom in question screamed simplistic, there is an area of the carpet left open for the children to sit on whilst the rest of the room is setup with tables and chairs. Upon the walls are several colourful display boards to illustrate the work of the children in different topics, a whiteboard and an interactive board are placed by the teacher's desk at the front of the class. Sat at the front of the class was an older looking woman.

'Hello, I'm Frances Garnham, I'm your new teaching assistant,' Frances called softly from the door.

As the woman turned, Frances was met with sharp facial features, hair pulled into a tight secure bun and formal clothing of a starch white shirt and a vintage tweed skirt; giving Frances the general idea of what a Victorian teacher would have looked like. She shuffled from one foot to the other as the teacher scrutinised her from head to toe.

'Caroline Macintosh. You seem awfully young.'

'Oh, well... Um... Yes. I'm twenty-four years old but I have had experience - '

'Are you qualified?' Caroline interrupted.

Frances gasped in disbelief. 'Of course, I'm qualified! I do have a degree in teaching,' she stammered in response.

With another judgemental glance Caroline stood up from her chair and strode across the room towards the door. 'Well, if you are here to work, you can start by clearing the display boards.' And with that, she was gone.

With an exasperated sigh, Frances set down her things and set about working on the display boards. She got the feeling this was going to be an awfully long school year.

***

Frances stored the display items into the correct piles in accordance with the topics. At this point the classroom door opened, and a young brunette girl walked in, she was slightly younger than Frances because her outfit suggested that she was keeping up to date with the recent fashion trends; unlike Frances who strived for comfort over *Vogue*. Frances discovered that this girl was Harper Craig-Lawson who was a student teacher working alongside Miss Macintosh in year one.

'So, what made you choose to become a teaching assistant when you have a teaching degree?' Harper asked.

'You could probably answer that question yourself when you graduate,' laughed Frances. 'My teaching degree made me realise that it's an overwhelming occupation. There's no work-life balance; you've really got to be thick-skinned to work in this profession.'

'Thanks for that,' Harper laughed as she pulled her shoulder length hair into a low bun.

'Oh, I am sure you will be fine! I am sure you could run rings around some people here, where was it you said that you studied?'

'Oxford, but that was a science degree, I am now doing my teacher training here in Lincoln,' Harper proudly stated.

'So why the change from science to teaching?' Frances puzzled. 'Surely you would get a more expanded career choice with science?'

'I always wanted to go into teaching, but I loved science throughout school, so I thought I could take my science speciality into schools by being a science subject lead.'

'Now that is logical,' Frances remarked. 'Having that end goal in mind will help you to stay in the teaching profession, you've got drive and a focus that's exactly what schools are looking for.'

'Well, I hope so,' Harper sighed. 'Anyway, chatting about my plans won't help me graduate and these lessons plans won't write themselves.' And with that Harper grabbed her things and made her way to the corner of the room near the teacher's desk and set about tapping away on her laptop.

***

It was nearing the end of the day and by this point Frances had taken down the old and put up the new displays and was now printing and trimming down resources as requested by Caroline.

'So Caroline are there any specific children you would like me to work with during lessons, perhaps in a small group?' Frances enquired. She wanted to show Caroline that she was capable and so wanted to help as much as possible with the class.

Caroline stared at Frances in confusion. 'And why would you need to do that Miss Garnham? Are you assuming the children won't understand my teaching? That I am not good at my job?'

'Oh no not at all Caroline! It's just that you haven't told me anything about the class I will be working with, and I thought that I could provide extra support to any children who might struggle with their learning?'

Caroline's face set into a glare. Frances' face became very pale.

'Now let's make one thing clear here Miss Garnham. You may have done your teacher training recently, but I have had far more experience of teaching in schools, and I will not be made to feel threatened in my classroom. I am the teacher here, so you follow by my teaching techniques. If a child does not understand the lesson that is because they are distracted and are not listening due to their unruly behaviour. The class seems to be mischievous from what I have seen of them anyway so need to be disciplined, not to follow the foolish methods you new teachers claim to use by giving them the power to run free and cause chaos. Just remember your place here, you are just a teaching assistant, and your role is to change the displays, prepare and handout any resources and paperwork. That way you will be able to watch how teaching is done from an expert. Do you understand?'

'O-oh um... of course Miss Macintosh, I'm sorry if I overstepped the mark,' a flustered Frances stuttered.

'Well now you know the expectations for future reference. But I will be watching you Miss Garnham and I warn you, if I do not feel that you are up to the standards set here in year one, then I will have no choice but to speak to Mrs Stevenson and have you removed.'

Abrupt Assassination…

Frances arrived at eight am the following morning, ready for an inset day full of meetings and getting acquainted with other colleagues. She didn't need to be in till half past eight, but she thought if she came in earlier, she might be able to get into Caroline's good book. With a travel cup in hand carrying the dregs of a cold cup of tea Frances psyched herself up to put on her positive work mindset, which was already running low and it was only day two, and headed into the school.

Plastering on a cheery smile Frances opened the door to the classroom and there of course was Caroline sitting at her desk studying paperwork which was laid out in carefully constructed piles.

'Good morning, Miss Macintosh. How are you?' Frances called as cheerily as she could manage.

'Very well Miss Garnham thank you,' sighed Caroline. 'It's good to see that you have adhered to our conversation yesterday and arrived early this morning.'

'Thank you, I just wanted to make a good impression,' Frances responded with a simple shrug and a smile.

'...Indeed,' Caroline replied blankly before turning her focus back onto the paperwork.

Frances quickly dropped her bags off into the little cupboard to the side of the classroom and set off with her travel mug to the classroom door. 'Well, I am going to grab a quick drink before the first meeting starts. I am looking forward to meeting the other staff members today.'

'Huh, I wouldn't be too sure about them,' snorted Caroline. 'Half of them don't know the meaning of the word discipline. I will be surprised if some of them last here for very much longer, some of the children are completely uncontrollable.'

'Oh right... good start,' Frances muttered under her breathe. 'Well, I will see you in the hall for the meeting.' And with that Frances escaped.

***

Whilst hiding from Caroline in the staffroom, Frances managed to meet some of the other members of staff who were grabbing another fresh cup of liquid energy before heading into the first of many tedious meetings. First Frances met Alice McKenzie, the reception teacher. Alice is an average height, smartly dressed blue eyed young woman whose blonde hair is either down or pulled back into a ponytail. Alice is very new to her teaching career but is extremely friendly and determined to continue teaching for years to come. Grant Kennedy was introduced as the year five teacher. With his black hair, brown eyes and knitted tank top which gives him the appearance of a nerd, Grant came across as a normal person who doesn't seem to be very talkative; he only stopped to give enough time for a brief but awkward introduction to Frances before scurrying away.

Grace and Dylan were soon added into the congregation beginning to form in the staffroom. Grace and Dylan were also both teaching assistants. Grace Taylor, grey haired with kind eyes, works within year four. The loving lines of life etched gracefully within the softened features of her face and warming smile shares that she has vast experiences from a well-lived life and loves her job, always being on hand to provide the other members of staff with a well needed boost which she emphasised to Frances with a reassuring squeeze on the shoulder. The year six teaching assistant was Dylan Walker, a larger-than-life person, he seemed an enthusiastic being who throws themselves into everything and already had Frances in fits of laughter after only having met him five minutes ago. He did try to pull off the sensible look by wearing a shirt and tie, but this had no impact on Dylan.

The four colleagues were getting on really well providing Frances with a run down on how the school works, information that Adeline had missed out on during the tour, but that must have been because a lot of the new information involved the hidden chocolate stash in the kitchen cupboard the teachers relied on after a painstakingly tiresome day which is why it was needing to be restocked constantly, plus the secret cupboard next to the entrance of the staffroom that was used by the cleaner and caretaker to store equipment and products but was the best place to have a private breakdown.

During the midst of these conversations the group were sent into a hush by the squeak coming from the opening of the staffroom door, Frances turned to see who caused the disruption. Stood in the door frame was a tall, thin man slightly balding on top with prominent features, beady eyes wearing waistcoat and trousers in a questionable tweed pattern. He peered at the group with a suspicious glare.

'Ah good morning, Ian lovely morning isn't it? Have you met Frances?' Grace cheerfully called, gesturing to Frances as a small introduction.

'Hello nice to meet you,' Frances smiled and gave a small wave to Ian.

Ian Marshall inspected Frances slowly, wearing a serious look as if he had a bad smell underneath his nose. 'Good morning,' Mr Marshall bluntly replied, and with a final browse around the room and at the four adults who were paralysed to the spot with a worried look on their faces from fear of what could follow, Ian Marshall made a coffee and stalked out of the room with his nose in the air.

'Well, he seems a barrel of laughs,' Frances murmured as she glanced at a smirking Dylan who replied with a shrug.

'Don't worry about him, Ian just thinks he is better than most people here. I think the only person he seems to have common ground with is Caroline,' He responded.

'Yeah but even they have their moments. Christ, I have never heard two people argue so much, and it's always about who knows best. They both think they're know-it-alls. They are always competing with each other,' Alice agreed as she rolled her eyes.

'Anything else you want to share with me whilst I still have time to escape?' Frances cried with an obvious hint of sarcasm.

'Afraid not, you are trapped with us now, there's no escaping here!' Grace chuckled. The group shared a final laugh as they collected their drinks and laptops before agreeing it was time to head to the hall.

***

Whilst settling into the hall waiting for the training to start, Frances had the opportunity to meet the other staff members. Frances was briefly introduced to the year four teacher Agatha Davidson. In her late thirties, Agatha's appearance matches her personality with her extremely curly hair colourful clothes, nails and makeup; her cheerful and welcoming handshake was accompanied with the sound of loud jangling bangles. Grace informed Frances that Agatha is as casual with her teaching as she is with her lifestyle, which is very casual indeed. She does have a great sense of humour and doesn't care to be involved in conflict, but she is a very open person and can be known to say things without thinking.

Charlotte Thompson was pointed out to Frances as the year six teacher, at a young twenty-nine, Charlotte has long brunette hair which is currently contained in an intricate hairstyle and is smartly dressed in a knee-length work dress. As she glanced towards their table, Frances saw Charlotte's blue eyes which seemed to be full of knowledge and novels, which seems to mirror Charlotte's personality. Charlotte was described by Grace as being academically minded and if she is not teaching or marking, she is likely to have her head in a book; she is very well spoken and always has an academic logical answer however socialising is not Charlotte's thing.

Finally, Frances was introduced to Lennox and Mildred Campbell who were bringing in the cake and biscuits Mildred had rustled up the night before to help give the staff an extra boost of sugar during their long tedious day training.

'So have you both been working here for long?' Frances asked through a mouthful of streusel cake as the staff were waiting for Adeline to get her head around the technology that was setting up the interactive whiteboard.

'Ha, almost as long as we have been married,' Lennox chortled.

'And we hope that will be for years to come,' Mildred cooed, gently placing a hand on Lennox's chest as she glanced at him affectionately.

'Wow! You must really love working here then?'
Frances pushed on, not wanting to witness the love
scene in front of her any further.

'Oh yes! The school is lovely, but that's all down to
the staff here, Mrs Stevenson selects only the best.
And the children are just delightful!' Mildred sung.

'Mm… a couple of scallywags here and there but
nothing like a bit of banter to keep them on side,'
Lennox agreed with a small nudge towards Frances.

Frances smiled as she took in a look at the couple in
front of her; they reminded her of her own
grandparents who she used to frequently visit as a
child. The couple both had soft and well-worn
features, which matched their casual clothing and
grey hair. The only difference between the two was
that one carried the smell of roses, the other carried
the smell of must. It wasn't difficult for Frances to
work out which fragrance matched Mildred and
Lennox.

Frances didn't have any more time to speak to
Mildred or Lennox because a tapping noise came
from the front of the hall as Adeline graciously

strolled to the edge of the first row of tables set out for the staff. 'Well apologies for the hold up, Amanda was going to have everything set up for me, but she must have gotten caught up in something else. Anyhow, now everything is sorted, and we are all here, let's not waste any more time!'

'Um, sorry to interrupt Adeline but not everyone is here,' Charlotte called from the back table. 'Caroline isn't here.'

'Oh,' Adeline replied as she glanced around the room, searching the small crowd seated in front of her. 'Well not to worry too much Charlotte as Frances is here so I am sure you can take notes for Caroline, right Frances?' Adeline responded looking over at Frances with a slight distressed look about her.

Frances nodded. 'Yes of course,' she replied reaching for a notebook and pen.

'Fabulous! Now let's crack on!'

Indeed, something did crack at that moment, but it wasn't Adeline it was the door to the hall opening. There in the doorway stood Harper, slightly panting.

'She must have been running late this morning,' thought Frances, pleased she had gotten here earlier than necessary because by the look on Adeline's face lateness isn't tolerated.

'Miss Craig-Lawson, you must be aware by now after spending the last term at our school that I do not appreciate my staff turning up as and when they please.'

Harper stood there, still panting and looking terrified, Frances felt sorry for her.

'Well as you are here now did you happen to see Miss Macintosh on your way here?' Mrs Stevenson curtly enquired.

Harper didn't answer, but instead Frances noticed her eyes grew wider at the name and her bottom lip seemed to be trembling. Frances slowly stood up as though to make her way over to Harper; but she didn't need to move as it seemed Adeline had too noticed the change.

'Harper, what's the matter dear?' Adeline gently probed, placing a hand on the girl's shoulder.

'I... um...she's-she's in the classroom,' Harper stammered. 'I think you'd better come and look,' she cried and charged out of the hall down the corridor. A commotion followed as all the staff were soon racing down the hallway asking each other questions about what may have happened to Caroline Macintosh...

'She was like this when I found her,' she whispered standing by the teacher's desk in the classroom.

One by one the staff entered. The classroom seemed all in order to Frances as she first walked in, but as she crept further into the room there seemed to be a pungent smell in the air, catching in her throat which she was sure wasn't there when she arrived earlier on in the day. She could hear other teachers stifling their coughs too, so she knew she wasn't the only one who had been affected by it.

A chill ran down Frances' spine which she noticed was brought on through the open windows, something else that again Frances was sure had changed since she had been in the room. But these didn't seem to matter once she heard the scream that came from Mildred.

As she edged towards the crowd forming round the teacher's desk. There was Adeline crouched over Caroline who was lying face down on the floor underneath the whiteboard. She looked a deathly pale white, mouth open with eyes full of terror… almost as if Caroline was struggling and feared for her life.

'Call an ambulance, quickly!' Screamed Adeline as she gently shook Caroline, hoping to wake her from a dream. Or a nightmare.

'I think we're too late,' Max muttered.

'No don't be ridiculous! This kind of thing doesn't happen in a school,' Mildred howled.

Unfortunately, by the time the ambulance had arrived, Max's fears had been confirmed.

Caroline Macintosh was pronounced dead.

Time of death - Nine am.

Difficult Detectives and Investigations Begin…

By ten am there was blue and white tape stretched across every doorway and tape flapping in the wind gripped around the gates, highlighting the monstrosity that had taken place there. Due to the commotion and flashing lights travelling through the tranquil village, people were peering through the village school gates; faces pressed between the bars hoping for a glimpse of gossip.

Inside the school, the staffroom is the only room the staff are allowed in. There is a solemn atmosphere. Frances secreted herself in the corner of the room out of the way. She glanced about the room to gauge the reactions of those around her to the distressing discovery this morning. Alice McKenzie is sat pale faced being comforted by Lennox Campbell who seems to have switched onto autopilot after the discovery. Agatha Davidson is currently walking tentatively from the small kitchen to the small two-seater sofa against the far wall carrying two strong cups of tea, one of which she passes to Harper.

'Here you are dear, there's extra sugar in there for the shock,' Agatha soothed.

Harper seemed to be away with it, as if on another planet, the look from earlier on this morning still plastered across her face... but there seemed to be an element of guilt slowly creeping into her eyes. She locked eyes with Frances, gave her a small smile and then looked away.

Ian Marshall was sat quietly drinking a coffee, there was no sense of change about him with the same look he had earlier, it seemed rather strange to Frances. Dylan was trying to calm and reassure a hysterical Amanda, he gave a desperate look of plea to Grace when he had done everything he could to no avail, Grace then came over to give him a helping hand. Amanda, whose mascara-stained face was soaked with tears, was howling which seemed to be the only noise filling the deathly silent staffroom. Amanda was currently reminding Frances slightly of *Alice Cooper*, not that Frances would share that.

Charlotte sat on a singular padded chair in her own corner of the room. She looked grave by the whole situation but also seemed as though she was thinking about something, almost reflecting. She seemed to be avoiding everyone else in the room, looking over at the hollering Amanda Morrison with a look of embarrassment. Frances felt that the anti-social side of Charlotte was implying that this was not the kind of place she wanted to be in right now. Mildred couldn't seem to keep still as though keeping busy will distract her mind from the devastation that happened earlier on in the day.

The only two people left in the room were Max and Grant. Frances glanced over at the pair and pondered over the activity of the two men. They were huddled in a corner in deep conversation, occasionally glancing at different people in the room. It was almost like they were playing their own murder mystery, examining the suspects one by one.

All of a sudden, Adeline came storming in looking dazed and overwhelmed. 'Um, apologies everyone for the long wait, but I have been speaking to the police and... unfortunately the police have requested that no one is to leave the school for now,' Adeline started. It did seem that Adeline was going to say more but she didn't get time to because a commotion broke out from the other staff, displaying their outrage at the situation. Adeline managed to seize the outbreak with a swift motion of her hand before continuing. 'I understand that this is not ideal and is very frustrating, but my hands are tied I'm afraid it's by orders from the detectives,' Adeline sounded very defeated as she raked a hand through her hair. She looked as though she needed a cup of tea, or something stronger, and a sit down. The room sensed Adeline's tension and the fact that she seemed to be on the brink of tears, and so remained silent for the rest of their imprisonment.

After what felt like an age of being cooped up, the door slowly crept open and in walked two gentlemen. One man was short, very short. He brought with him the look of a farmer with his bushy top lip moustache, and his fashion sense seemed to consist of different shades of brown judging from his three-piece suit and trench coat. The man with him seemed to be the complete opposite. He was tall with brown hair, his fresh face told Frances he was younger than his counterpart. It was his understanding eyes and charming smile that made Frances think that he was someone she could get along with. The older man pulled himself up to as much height as he could muster and scanned the room and the confused, exhausted faces staring back at him.

'Good morning, everyone. I'm Detective Chief Inspector Barry Hughes from the M.I.T,' he announced proudly showing off his police badge. 'And this is my colleague Detective Inspector Jonathan Birch.'

'Hello, I'm um… terribly sorry for your loss,' Birch raised his hand as a small welcoming to the group as he was introduced.

'Mm… yes well, moving on. I have spoken with your headmistress Mrs Stevenson, and we have arranged a small room in which I would like to ask you all a couple of questions,' Hughes sniffed.

'Woah woah hold up. Why are you questioning us?' Dylan called out.

'Surely you don't think it was one of us?' Amanda exclaimed as her lower lip trembled.

'At the minute Madam until we can gauge more of an idea of what happened and until everyone is questioned,' he paused dramatically, holding a gaze with everyone in the room as he continued. 'You are all suspects.'

'Suspects? How do you know it was murder?' Charlotte interjected, raising an eyebrow at Hughes.

'We are covering all scenarios Miss, until we are positive as to what caused Miss Macintosh's death.'

It seemed to Frances that he was enjoying the blame game he had just started.

'Very well if we are to be interrogated like criminals, I shall be in my classroom when you need me Chief Inspector. I have lessons to plan,' Ian huffed as he made his way towards the door. Ian was metres away from the entrance when he was ground to a halt by the stout policeman.

'Unfortunately, Sir that will not be possible. To ensure everyone stays on the premises, all the rooms can be checked, and the crime scene is not tampered with, I am requesting that you are all to stay in here until the scene of the crime has been examined and you have all been accounted for.'

'You can't be serious!' Grant fumed as he raked his hand through his hair.

'You cannot command us to sit in here all day, what exactly do you expect us to do. We have work that needs doing.' Charlotte fired at the two policemen.

At this point Amanda started frantically scanning the room hyperventilating. Jonathan moved towards her whispering soothing reassurances, it took Hughes all the effort in his body not to roll his eyes and call out some smart remark about her being kept in a staffroom at a school, not being trapped in an escape room!

Adeline, who hadn't uttered a word since the detectives had arrived in the staffroom and now realising she wasn't handling this in the way a headteacher should be dealing with the situation, suddenly rushed over to Chief Inspector Hughes to negotiate a deal. 'Surely the teachers can go into their classes to collect their things under supervision. I think being able to work would help to provide a distraction for them.'

With a disgruntled sigh, Chief Inspector Barry agreed that the rooms had to be examined and once clear, the staff would be escorted into their rooms to collect their things before being brought back into the staffroom.

After a while the workforce were once again seated in the staffroom, only this time the sound was laptop keys tapping away instead of silence or Amanda's wailing. No one spoke or even interacted with each other, the only time eyes left the screens was when someone returned from questioning with the same foggy expression they left with and no new answers.

***

At long last Frances got called in for her round of questioning. She walked into the headteacher's office. It felt smaller than the last time Frances was in there, she couldn't work out if that was because there were detectives in there now not just one friendly headteacher, or if it was because she felt like the world was slowly closing in due to the morning's events. But either way there she was now, sitting opposite two police detectives wondering what the hell has happened. Before she could travel deeper down her tunnel of thoughts, she was snatched back into reality with a cough from Chief Inspector Hughes, and so with that the questioning had begun.

'So, Miss Garnham, I understand you haven't been working here for very long,' Hughes started.

''Frances please, um yes, I only started here yesterday. My plan was to meet the staff and find my way around the school before the children arrived for the start of term tomorrow.'

'Mhm, and how did you find the staff?'

'Very welcoming, most have welcomed me with open arms.'

'Most? Does this include Caroline Macintosh?'

'Well, I don't think Caroline and I really saw eye to eye-'

'In what way?' Hughes interrupted.

'Well, we had different ideas on my role and opinions on discipline. But I was happy to support in Caroline's classroom and go by her rules,' Frances innocently responded.

Hughes nodded slowly, glancing at a frantic Jonathan Birch who was furiously scribbling in his notebook ensuring to capture all the evidence. 'Did you get all that Birch?' He grilled.

'Er, yes sir,' came the feeble response. Frances got the feeling that Birch hadn't been doing this job for very long and was still trying to get into his boss' good book.

'Good. And where were you this morning just before the death was announced Miss Garnham,' the detective continued turning his focus back to the interview in progress.

'I was in the hall, waiting for the training to start.'

'Did you see Caroline at all before that?' Jonathan enquired, there was a split second when his faced showed a sense of pride that he had managed to ask a question, but that soon disappeared when he saw the glare he was receiving from his boss.

'Uh yes, I did. I came into the classroom in the morning to drop off my bags. Caroline was in there. We had a brief conversation and then I left the classroom to get a drink in the staffroom before training started in the hall. I met Alice McKenzie, Grace Taylor, Dylan Walker and I briefly saw Grant Kennedy and Ian Marshall in there and then we all left to head for the hall together-'

'And what time did you leave Miss Macintosh?' Questioned Barry.

'I arrived at eight, so it must have been about quarter past eight,' Frances mused.

'And you didn't see her after that at all?' Jonathan quizzed.

'No, I didn't see her after that.'

'Right... Very well Miss Garnham. As you are aware you are still unable to leave the premises so you may return to the staffroom. And we will be in touch if we have any more questions for you.' Barry concluded.

'Thank you, Chief Inspector Hughes and Detective Inspector Birch,' Frances nodded at the policemen and headed towards the door. Only she paused when she got to the door frame, there was something niggling at her, something she needed to know. She turned back to face the men who were currently reading through their notes.

'Um, sorry it's not my place to ask but have you got any idea as to how Caroline died?' Frances asked quietly.

Barry Hughes looked up. 'As of yet no, but I am sure there is a reasonable explanation. Natural death perhaps,' was the very blasé response.

The expression on Frances' face was only noticed by Jonathan who enquired, 'Is everything okay Miss Garnham?'

Frances sighed, throwing her arms in the air. 'I think it seems odd. There was no weapon and...

how does a teacher die in a primary school?' She pondered aloud.

'Well, you have no need to think about it anymore Miss, you can leave it to those qualified to deal with this kind of situation. And besides nobody has announced this death as murder so there is no need to overreact, Miss Macintosh may have had an underlying illness which caused her death, nothing to it really,' Hughes responded brusquely.

Slightly flabbergasted by the response from the small man Frances gave a quick nod as recognition and left, not that her reaction mattered because Barry was already once again deep in paperwork; only Jonathan Birch saw the whole thing and was now feeling a level of sympathy for Frances and awkwardness when replaying Barry's interviewing technique and responses to Frances' questions in his mind.

Frances' brain was working on overdrive as she was walking back to the staffroom:

How did Caroline die when there was no weapon?

Could it be an accident?

Natural death?

People don't just drop dead in their fifties!

What if it wasn't an accident?

But why would someone want to murder a primary school teacher?

Who would want Caroline dead?

Something wasn't sitting right with Frances and Hughes' response to her question earlier didn't reassure her in any way. He seemed too relaxed and at ease about it all, as if it was an open and shut case. Something had to be done, and maybe Frances was the ideal person to do so. Frances knew no one, she could easily slip under the radar and put questions to the other staff without causing any suspicion. And Jonathan seemed to be very friendly, Frances was sure she could wiggle some additional information out of him.

'This could work,' she thought. 'I have to do something; things like this don't happen in primary schools.' Frances wouldn't rest until the truth around Caroline's mysterious death was unveiled. 'Surely there's nothing wrong with a little snooping,' she decided with a smile. 'Just a little bit.' Although she hoped she wouldn't be needing any little grey cells or knitting needles to help her.

Colleague Clashes and Many Motives…

Frances tried to drag out the walk back to the staffroom, she wanted to work through the thoughts in her head before having to face the continuous questioning from those hidden away in the staffroom. In order to elongate her walk, Frances decided to stroll by the scene of the crime, with the thought that her investigation should start by looking over the place where it all seemed to go wrong. Expecting the door to be barricaded with police, Frances was astonished to find no one there, not a single officer. They must have been on a very long lunch. Sensing a stroke of luck which shouldn't be missed, Frances cautiously crept into the classroom.

Casting her mind back to the discovery of Caroline Macintosh, Frances tried to remember how the scene had been laid out before her. The window which was open earlier causing a chill in the air had since been tightly closed, and the overpowering smell had now disappeared. It was almost as if Frances had imagined it. The body of Caroline was no longer there, but the yellow evidence markers covered where Caroline once laid. Glancing up, the writing was still on the board, Frances could see where Caroline had abruptly stopped scribing. She just couldn't understand how someone managed to be completely fine in the morning and be dead a few hours later without leaving anything behind. Or did Macintosh plan this herself?

Frances was searching for the whiteboard pen she was sure it was by Caroline's body, but it seemed to have miraculously disappeared, when she was interrupted by a cry from the door.

'Hey! You're not allowed in here Miss!'

Frances jumped up with wide eyes to be met with a startled yet cross police officer.

'Oh... um... I'm terribly sorry, I-I-I was just looking for some... scissors! Ah! Here we are, that's great. So sorry again,' Frances blagged as she quickly grabbed the scissors and stumbled to the door. She didn't need the scissors, but unfortunately Frances was never good at lying and this was the best excuse she could come up with in the spur of the moment.

Frances flew down the corridor and back into the staffroom where she spent the rest of the afternoon.

***

The news was announced Wednesday morning. The news travelled further through the papers, radio and news programmes. Soon the picturesque town was buzzing with noise, reporters were huddled outside the school gates ready to pounce hoping for inside knowledge from a member of staff trapped in the school.

The school temporarily closed to allow time for the police to complete their investigation and for the staff to grieve. The teachers were back in the school though, despite the tragic events, in order to distribute work for the children to complete at home.

Frances found the school eerily silent and uncomfortable to work in, it was as though Frances was stuck in a ghost town. She was making her way to the staffroom. She was in need of a hot cup of tea to help her work through sorting all the documents before sending them over to the children she had never met; and with no Harper here she was on her own. She needed something to get her through, so a cup of tea it was. Upon arriving in the staffroom, Frances found Adeline in the small kitchen making what looked like a strong black coffee.

'Good morning, Mrs Stevenson how are you? Sorry, I didn't realise you were in here.' Frances could guess how Adeline was, the dark circles forming under her eyes and the grim expression plastered across her face suggested that Adeline had very little sleep and was not thrilled to be here.

'Oh, good morning Frances, please don't apologise. I am just preparing a rather big pick-me-up to brace myself for today,' Adeline sighed as she gestured to her large coffee cup.

'Is everything okay?' Frances queried nervously, slowly edging towards the kitchen side and placing her own mug down.

'Well, it is as okay as it can be given the circumstances,' the headteacher gave a small smile and a shrug. 'I have to write a speech today to present in front of the press. And I just don't know what to say. It's not something you ever think you will have to write, is it?' Adeline shared, resting her chin on her hand.

'Oh, I had no idea,' Frances inwardly kicked herself. 'No, I suppose it isn't. I am sure the words will come flowing through, you must have known Caroline for a few years so you must have had a strong work relationship. There must be an awful lot of memories to reminisce on,' Frances suggested trying to give a positive view to Adeline's obvious bleak outlook.

Adeline made a guilty face. 'In all honesty, Caroline and I never really had a work relationship.'

'Oh,' Frances squeaked.

'Caroline was very formal and reserved with her conversations. The only conversations I had with her were when she tried to give her opinion on how I should be running the school, which was very often but I didn't take any notice. Caroline and I had very different ideas about running a school,' Adeline stated as a matter of fact.

'Ah I see.'

'Oh, don't get me wrong, we were always civil towards each other,' Adeline stumbled frantically. 'And I wouldn't ever wish anything on Caroline… it's just an unfortunate turn of events,' she ended as she stared out the window.

'Indeed,' Frances agreed, following Adeline's gaze out onto the empty playground. There was then a brief moment of contemplation between the two, as if the pair still needed time to get their heads around what had happened.

'Anyway,' Adeline shook her head snapping back into reality. 'Can't just stand here I suppose, must get on.'

'Yes of course, well I hope the speech goes well. I am sure you will find the right words,' Frances heartened.

'Thank you, Frances and thank you for helping sort out Caroline's class, I really do appreciate it. And if you need any help, we are more than happy to give you a helping hand.'

'Anytime Adeline, anything I can do to help. If I need any help, I will be sure to ask.'

And with that Adeline and Frances made their drinks and made their way out of the staffroom and off on their own individual tasks.

***

Halfway through the morning Frances needed to collect some paperwork off the printer, which is where she met Amanda.

'Hello Amanda, glad to see you are feeling… better today.' Amanda's mascara covered face flashed into Frances' mind.

'Hiya honey, thank you! Thank God for makeup, I barely slept a wink last night! Still can't get my head around it all,' Amanda gasped.

'I know what you mean. It's a shame really, I never really got to know Caroline.'

'Ha! Don't worry, you weren't missing out on much there,' Amanda snorted.

'What do you mean?' Frances asked, sounding sceptical.

'Caroline was a stuffy cow. She thought I was a busy body and an airhead; she was so rude! Whenever Caroline saw me talking to other members of staff, she would think I was gossiping and would roll her eyes,' Amanda complained.

'Oh no!' Frances cried, from Amanda's response to Caroline's death yesterday, this wasn't the outburst she was expecting.

'Honestly, she was a nightmare! She would criticise my looks, telling me I had too much makeup on or that I should get rid of my claws or caterpillars. What the hell did she mean by that?' Amanda continued, there was part of Frances that thought Amanda was partly enjoying moaning about Caroline. There was another part of Frances that had to stop herself from smiling over Caroline referring to Amanda's false eyelashes as caterpillars and her fake nails as claws. If there was one thing

Frances and Caroline seemed to have in common, it was their sense of humour. It was a shame in Frances' opinion that she would never get to see that for herself.

'It seems like Caroline had an opinion on a lot of things then?' Frances remarked as she flicked through the printed papers.

'Silly cow should have minded her own business and stuck to teaching, otherwise she would have had to deal with the consequences sooner or later.' The room went silent. Frances looked up from her paperwork shocked. Amanda quickly clamped her mouth shut and her eyes widened. 'Oh... I-I-I.... I-I wouldn't have done anything obviously! I wouldn't hurt Caroline of course!' Amanda stammered.

Silence filled the room again. Luckily Amanda was saved from digging herself into a bigger hole by the phone ringing. Without a second thought, Amanda charged over to the desk chair and glided across the floor, grabbing the phone off the receiver. 'Good morning, Arrows Primary Academy, this is Amanda the receptionist speaking how may I help you?' She greeted the caller as professionally as she could muster. Frances was impressed with how that rolled off the tongue. Both Amanda and Frances seemed relieved for the opportunity to escape the awkward conversation. So Frances took her paperwork, gave Amanda a small smile which was returned and headed off to the classroom.

***

During the afternoon Frances took a wander around the school as a break from sorting and emailing paperwork. Her walk took her to the reception classroom, where she found Alice tapping away on her laptop at her desk. Frances can't have crept up as quietly as she had thought because Alice looked up and greeted Frances with a cheery smile.

'Hello! Are you alright or have you got lost?' Alice joked as she closed her laptop lid.

'Very funny!' Frances chortled. 'No, I decided to have a little wander around, I needed to get away from my laptop and get out of the silent classroom. Although it seems just as quiet in the whole school as it does in the classroom, where is everyone?'

'I know it's like a ghost town! I don't think people are up for a lot of conversation today plus, all this work prep for the children is keeping everyone locked up in their rooms,' Alice suggested turning on her desk chair to face Frances. 'Don't worry, it isn't normally like this. It is normally a buzz of activity with people everywhere!'

'Well, that's alright then! At least it won't be like this for much longer! So, you must have had lots of conversations with Caroline then, especially about the children moving into her class?' Frances mused, resting against the classroom door.

'Ah in all honesty, the complete opposite. I actually tried to avoid conversations with Caroline. I have been known to walk the long way round back to my classroom just to avoid meeting her!'

'Really! Why? Was she that bad?' Frances sounding surprised.

'It might just be me, but she scared me! She always had very harsh views about how we teach. But then again, she irritated me because she always felt the need to share her opinions in every conversation, even when we didn't ask for them,' Alice rested her head against her hand.

Frances slowly nodded her head and turned to her own thoughts. She knew Alice wasn't the only one with this opinion as she had similar responses from Adeline and Amanda, and she was assuming that they wouldn't be the last with that opinion.

'I guess I don't have to worry about that anymore,' Alice murmured quietly into the silent room. At that comment Frances looked up. She was surprised that Alice would say that, like she was relieved Caroline was gone. Alice met Frances' eyes and gave a simple shrug before saying: 'Anyway, best get on!' She turned to her laptop again and tapped away at the keys. Frances nodded, taking the hint that the conversation was over, and took a slow walk back to the classroom.

Frances spent the next couple of hours sending out work and answering parent's queries, trying not to mention Caroline as much as possible. She had just sent a rather detailed email to a difficult parent when suddenly the door opened. Frances looked up to see a smiley Agatha waving at her.

'Hello! Only me! I just wanted to pop in and check how you were getting on and if you needed anything.'

'Hi! I'm getting on alright thank you, just sent off the last of the children's work and have just been answering some emails. But I am so glad to see another face around here, it's been so empty,' Frances sighed as she stretched back in her chair raising her arms above her head. 'I was starting to think that people were avoiding this room!'

'Ha! Oh, bless you I don't think people are avoiding you, I think people are trying to get themselves organised. It was all so sudden; we are all trying to keep learning as the main focus to the children. I just can't believe it. I would never have imagined a body being discovered in a school! And it's such a shame, poor Caroline, nobody deserves that,' Agatha turned to last year's class picture hanging on the wall, looking at Caroline's stern face behind the last row of smiling pupils, as she perched on the edge of the tables.

Frances raised her eyebrows. 'Wow, I think that is the nicest thing I have heard someone say about

Caroline. All the people I have spoken to have said nothing but negative comments about her!'

'I am guessing a lot of people labelled her as opinionated?' Agatha quizzed.

Frances nodded. 'What made you say that?' She chuckled.

'Caroline would voice her views whenever she could. I admit I never agreed with them, but that's because our opinions were the complete opposite. She grew up in a different society to me so her childhood experiences were a lot different to mine. But I never argued with her, there was no point I wasn't going to change her mind plus there is no point in causing conflict between colleagues,' Agatha started.

'That's very diplomatic of you Agatha.'

'I know I do have my serious moments!' Agatha squealed; the pair chuckled. 'But in all seriousness despite Caroline's flaws, I admired her extensive years of teaching experience and for that I did respect Caroline and still do.'

'Aw, that's lovely Agatha, it's nice to hear that Caroline wasn't always seen as the villain.'

'Well, nobody's perfect, are they?' Agatha continues.

Frances just went to agree when suddenly two figures appeared at the door frame. Frances must have been so focused on the figures at the door because Agatha turned round to follow her gaze.

'Oh hello! What brings you two here?' Agatha called. The two figures turned out to be Grace and Dylan, who both seemed to be holding a large lunchbox each.

'Hello! We were coming to collect Frances for lunch,' Grace responded, waving her lunchbox. 'We can't have Frances slaving away and missing out on lunch, can we? How are you finding it all Frances? Managing to sort everything out alright?'

Frances looked at the clock on her laptop in disbelief. 'Oh god! Look at the time, I never thought about lunch, it completely slipped my mind! Yes, it's all fine Grace, all the work for today has been sent off so it's all good thank you. How have you been finding it all? I bet you had yours all sent off a lot earlier than I did,' Frances chuckled.

'Oh, you're joking right? Not only did Charlotte manage to send all of today's work off, but she has also started sorting out the work for the next few days as well! Christ, it's almost like Charlotte saw this happening in her crystal ball!' Dylan cried, pulling out a plastic chair and throwing himself into it.

'It's nice to see that Charlotte is organised. We've got all ours sorted alright didn't we Agatha?' Grace chipped in, sitting on the desk beside Dylan.

'We did indeed, I think we might start sorting out tomorrow's work this afternoon. Take a leaf out of Charlotte's book,' Agatha agreed, giving a sideways glance at Dylan who responded with an eye roll.

'Honestly, it would be like Caroline to make a dramatic exit and leave us in a mess like this. I bet she is smirking and gloating down there,' Dylan grumbled making a pointed gesture towards the floor.

'Dylan! That is an awful thing to say!' Grace gasped.

'Oh, don't you start feeling sorry for her now Grace,' Dylan retorted. 'I can't count how many times you used to moan to me about her!'

'That was only because she would always voice that absurd opinion of hers, some of her ideas about teaching were very similar to teaching in the Victorian era. It was horrific. And I wasn't the only one who found that,' Grace justified.

'No, it is true, that is a general consensus among the staff unfortunately,' Agatha agreed giving a sad nod.

'That still doesn't justify all the arguments you used to have,' Dylan pressed on. 'Honestly Frances the things they would say to each other, you would not believe-'

'Yes, alright Dylan, you've made your point!' Grace interrupted with a shriek. Frances turned to face Grace, hoping that she might get a little more insight into Grace's relationship with Caroline. At this point Frances had already gauged the relationships with Caroline from five different members of staff and she didn't need to probe them in anyway. Dylan also turned his gaze towards Grace, wearing a very proud and smug look. Grace responded with a threatening look in his direction before gaining her composure to continue with her explanation. 'Yes, we did argue often. But that was only because Caroline kept pestering me and making snide comments about me retiring. Her opinion was that I should retire because of my age, I would justify myself stating that age has nothing to do with it, I love working with children I work with, and I still have the same amount of passion as I did when I started this job. But that didn't stop her, so I decided to play her at her own game, well she was only three years younger than me! So, I told her that she should retire because her views were old-fashioned, you can imagine how well that went down,' Grace gave a slight chuckle. 'But that doesn't mean I would justify something awful happening to her. I wouldn't wish that upon anyone!'

'That's her guilty conscious creeping in,' Dylan joked tapping his temple.

'Oh, shut up you,' Grace snapped pushing him jokingly.

'I guess I don't need to ask how you felt towards Caroline eh Dylan?' Frances probed smugly trying to turn the conversation to Dylan.

'I don't know what you mean,' Dylan gasped giving Frances a hurt look. 'Yeah, Caroline and I did not get on.

'You don't say!' Agatha laughed.

'Well, we have… had completely different personalities. She thought I was a class clown, I thought she was boring. Caroline found me irritating and a nuisance, and I found her to be snobby. So, we didn't converse or interact with each other. We didn't give each other the time of day, made life easier really,' Dylan shrugged. Frances nodded in response; she wasn't surprised by Dylan's thoughts on Caroline. She couldn't picture Dylan and Caroline being the best of friends.

The room seemed to then fall silent. There wasn't much else to say, the views Frances had heard so far were very similar, and from her first interaction with Caroline she could understand why people felt that way. But it did make her feel uneasy about the cause of the sudden death of Caroline.

'Anyway,' Dylan broke the silence waving his lunchbox in the air. 'This food won't eat itself. Let's go take our minds off all this with lunch.' The group collected their things and with a murmured agreement, headed towards the staffroom.

Unfortunately for them, they didn't get the lunch break they had hoped for.

Dishing More Dirt and Information Identified…

Unfortunately, lunch in the staffroom wasn't as peaceful and relaxing as Dylan had planned it to be. Within minutes of arriving, conversation soon turned to the recent death of Caroline. Some jumped at the chance to share their opinions of the deceased quicker than others. That's where one person took the conversation.

'Frances has been asking about our thoughts on Caroline,' Dylan blurted during a pause in the chat.

Frances gave Dylan a look of horror. 'I am asking because I only had the brief encounter with Caroline the day before and the morning of her death. I was hoping to gain more of an insight about her from the people who have worked with her if you must know Dylan,' Frances remarked pointedly.

'Honestly Dylan, you make it sound as if Frances had an ulterior motive,' Agatha laughed.

'I mean it's perfectly understandable,' Max jumped in. 'At least Frances now knows how lucky she is that she didn't have to put up with Caroline for very long.'

'Ooh here we go!' Dylan called excitedly, rubbing his hands together in glee. 'Go on then Max! You get the ball rolling, tell Frances what she really was missing out on.'

Frances looked over to where Max was sitting, as a non-verbal cue for Max to join in the conversation. Max took this cue and came over to join the group.

'I just think as having been in the same Key Stage with her and therefore having had to have regular meetings with her, I think I am the most experienced on the topic of Caroline,' Max shrugged.

'How awful, we are now labelling Caroline as a topic of conversation rather than a person,' Grace exclaimed. The room fell silent for a few moments, contemplating Grace's words.

Someone soon broke the silence. 'Anyway, Max you were saying,' Dylan pushed moving nearer the edge of his seat. Max cleared his throat as Grace gave Dylan a tut of shame and rolled her eyes.

'Well as you know, Caroline and I planned lessons together. If I am honest, it was a miracle how I got through some of those meetings, they were tiresome and agitating. Caroline spent the majority of the meeting wittering on about how she was always right about anything and everything and that the new ways of teaching were ridiculous and completely wrong.'

'I can see why that would become monotonous,' Frances agreed, feeling a level of sympathy for Max. Having only known Caroline for approximately a day, she could understand why Max felt the way he did towards Caroline.

'If I am completely honest, the best thing would have been to have got rid of Caroline and replaced her with someone else,' Max responded flatly.

'Well, you have already got half that wish Max, all that is left is to find Caroline's replacement,' Dylan laughed.

'Oh, honestly Dylan, I don't think Max would plan for Caroline to leave in such an unfortunate way!' Mildred gasped, walking gingerly from the kitchenette towards the two-seater sofa with a steaming mug of tea in her hand.

'But he is right about one thing,' Lennox piped up. 'She don't belong in a primary school. Stuck up cow.'

'Lennox! You can't say that' Mildred blurted to her husband from across the room.

'Oh, come on love, she always looked down on us and made us feel unwelcome here. She was always up herself because she was posh. Plus, she never treated those little nippers right; over the years we have worked here she has always been a harsh woman. Some of those kids would come out of her classroom crying. Horrible woman,' Lennox defended himself leaning on the kitchen counter as he did so.

'That's terrible!' Frances cried as she wrapped her cardigan around her a bit tighter.

'It is,' Mildred agreed with a regretful sigh. 'But it is still an awful turn of events.'

'Indeed.' Came a voice from the corner of the room. Frances followed the voice to find Ian Marshall sat poised in the corner with the same arrogant look he had on his face the day Frances first met him. 'One of the last people in this school to know the real definition of discipline,' Ian continued giving a knowing look to the other teachers around him. 'Caroline and I were the firm hand this school needed to be where it is today.'

'Of course,' Max responded sarcastically. 'But I remember some of the snide remarks shared between yourself and Caroline from time to time.'

'Well, somebody had to keep Caroline grounded,' Ian retorted. 'I had to sometimes remind her that she wasn't the only one intelligent enough to have a degree.' Ian took a sip from his mug of coffee.

Dylan turned to make eye contact with Frances, he managed to sum up his thoughts on Ian's statement in the swift motion of raising one eyebrow followed by rolling his eyes. Frances tried to stifle a laugh. She also wanted to point out to Ian that everyone here also has a degree, but she felt this wasn't the time nor place so kept her mouth shut. At this point seeing as no one had the effort or time to argue with Ian, the room fell silent once again.

During the lull in conversation, Frances took a moment to look at the literal strangers around her. To her left in front of the kitchenette sat Lennox and Mildred hand in hand, reminding her of otters when they held hands whilst going to sleep to make sure neither of them drifted off into the sea. To her right sat Grace, Agatha and in the corner was Dylan, presumably sat in the naughty corner with a mischievous grin on his face whilst Grace and Agatha were quietly sat sipping at their hot beverage of choice. Across from her were Ian and Charlotte. Ian was sat with an air of authority about him, thinking back at his previous comments during the conversation then his pose really made sense. Meanwhile Charlotte was more hidden away on the chair behind the door with her head once again in what Frances could make out as a classic literature novel. The last two people in the room were Grant, who had positioned himself in the corner, whilst Max had placed himself next to Dylan when he came over to join in the conversation. Something suddenly came to Frances, a flashback. Max had moved from beside Grant to cross the room, her mind then cast back to the morning after the discovery of Caroline's body, both Max and Grant had stood in the same spot as they were earlier on today. It may have just been a coincidence, but then that morning they had been talking... looking suspicious.

'Perhaps not a coincidence?' Frances pondered to herself. She wasn't kept in her own thoughts for very long as a voice chimed in, no surprise as to who it was.

'What about you Grant? Charlotte? You've been very quiet. Care to share your thoughts?'

Grant glanced up at the sound of his name. 'Well unlike you Dylan, some of us don't like to get involved in all the drama.' Dylan threw himself back in his seat as he gave a hurt look dramatically at Grant who responded with a look of disapproval through raising a singular eyebrow at him. A few muffled chuckles filled the air. 'But since you asked. I hardly spoke to her and had very little interaction with her in all honesty.'

'Still doesn't tell us what you thought of her,' Dylan pushed further, receiving a slightly forceful whack on the arm from Agatha.

'Alright, from the very few interactions I have had with Caroline, I found her to be very conceited, up herself if you will. But like I say, I rarely spoke to her,' Grant ended his statement with a simple shrug.

'Oh …well that was…boring,' Dylan stated with a sigh full of disappointment. 'Your turn, what about you?' He turned towards Charlotte.

Getting a sense of someone watching her, Charlotte lifted her head to see several pairs of eyes on her. She slowly slid the bookmark back in between the pages and placed the book gently on her lap. 'And what exactly do you want to know?' Charlotte enquired, straight to the point.

'Well, we've all shared our thoughts on Caroline to the newbie,' Dylan explained, gesturing towards Frances as he spoke. 'It's only fair that you share your views on Caroline.'

'Oh, honestly you can't be serious Dylan this is ridiculous,' Grace cried out. 'Don't worry Charlotte dear, you don't have to say anything,' She tried reassuring Charlotte.

'Oh, come on why not? What harm can it do eh? To share our thoughts on Caroline? What's she gonna do, come back and haunt us?' Dylan interjected with a hint of humour. Obviously, no one else had the same sense of humour as Dylan because he was scolded by Grace and Agatha who shook their heads in disappointment.

'Very well if you must know, I didn't really socialise with Caroline a lot-' Charlotte began.

'Despite the fact I would walk in on you having an argument?' Dylan jumped in.

'We were not arguing, we were having a small dispute or a clash over academic views, insignificant things in fact. We only clashed because Caroline couldn't accept the fact that other people had opinions that were not the same or similar to hers,' Charlotte retorted back.

'You two sounded like the best of friends then,' Max joined in sarcastically, giving Frances a small jokey smirk. Frances gave a friendly chuckle in response. Charlotte, who was obviously not impressed by the sarcasm, threw Max an annoyed glare before responding.

'No, we weren't best friends, we weren't even friends for that matter. We were just work colleagues who were civil to each other when we did have to have a conversation,' Charlotte paused. 'But I do think that the best thing that could have happened to Caroline would be for her to have been taken down a peg or two.'

An uncomfortable silence filled the room, so uncomfortable that it made Frances want to curl up in a ball and hide under the table. Luckily for her, time seemed to slip by quicker than the congregation had anticipated, so the group dispersed and locked themselves in their own classrooms again. Frances spent the rest of the day setting up her paperwork to send out for the next day and responding to parents, which is definitely not how she wanted the first parent-teacher interaction to go.

At precisely four thirty pm, Frances packed up her things and raced across the car park to her car. The need to get out of the classroom was overwhelming, so the moment freedom called Frances took it. Whilst settling into the car and setting up her music playlist, Frances took some time to reflect on her findings from the day. She got a strong feeling that no one was a massive fan of Caroline, and strangely no one seemed too distraught over her death, which gave Frances an unnerving feeling. She was suddenly catapulted out of her seat as *The Drifters* came blaring out of the car speakers. Shaking off the unsettling feeling, she pulled off the handbrake put the car into drive and rolled out of the school car park out onto the silent country roads.

***

On Thursday, Frances was no longer trapped in solitary confinement as she was blessed with help from Harper. In order to fully prepare for the children's arrival back at school next week Harper had been called in to help give Frances a meticulous run down of the details of the children in the class; especially as it was decided that Harper and Frances would run the classroom until the interview process had been completed and a new teacher had been selected.

'So that's the basic rundown of the students,' Harper concluded as she packed up her notes and slipped them back into her bag. 'Of course, you will get to know more about their personalities as time goes on, but they are a really lovely class. How have you been finding all the class prep? Need a hand with any of the resources for next week?'

'I think we are all good on the prep front, but we can spend some time today trimming down all the worksheets, saves us a job to do later in the week. Everyone has been telling me that I have nothing to worry about with the class. I'm pretty sure Mildred has made it her daily mission to ease my anxiety by telling me that they are a class of thirty angels,' Frances chuckled flopping back into the desk chair as she twirled her hair around her hand before putting it into a bun using a hair clip. 'Not that I think Caroline would agree they seemed to be devils in her eyes with their unruly behaviour.'

Harper shook her head as she rested her feet on the edge of one of the desks. 'Well, that's Caroline for you. It's a shame really, I don't think she ever really saw those kids for what they were… just kids.'

Frances glanced over to Harper with a perplexed look. 'What were your thoughts on Caroline? If you don't mind me asking of course! I am just trying to gain an overall idea on what Caroline was like, doesn't seem a lot of the staff had a positive view on her unfortunately.'

Harper met Frances' eyes with a resigned look and sighed. 'I mean look credit where credit's due, I respect Caroline for the countless years she has spent in the teaching world I take on any advice she ever gave me, of course I did, she was my placement mentor!' Harper places her head in her hand and gave her head a gentle shake before continuing. 'However, I will admit I didn't always agree with her teaching views. I never liked the way she spoke to the children; she always spoke down to them, rarely used any praise. It took me back to how I was treated when I was at school. I hated it.'

'I'm so sorry you had to go through that. I'm terribly sorry I didn't want to bring up past memories, I should have kept my mouth shut,' Frances fumbled as she fiddled with her nails and thumbs. She felt awful for putting Harper in a situation where she had to open up, especially to someone she barely knew like Frances.

'Oh no don't worry about it! Honestly it was all going to come out at some point, and it was one of the reasons I wanted to become a teacher, I wanted to make sure that children aren't given the same experience I was given. I wanted children to be happy coming into the classroom not full of dread,' Harper responded with a determined smile.

Frances was in awe of Harper, for someone to have gone through such a horrible experience and use that to improve the lives of future generations was awe-inspiring. Frances didn't believe it was possible to be proud of someone you barely knew, but she was.

'That's amazing Harper. I am sure children will be lucky to have a teacher like you. It's a shame you and Caroline didn't see eye-to-eye, it must have made for an awkward atmosphere in the classroom.'

'Oh, don't get me wrong we may not have had the same views, but we never argued or had a disagreement, but that may have been because I never shared my views with Caroline. I don't think she would have paid attention to it anyway!' Harper chortled.

Frances had to agree, Caroline didn't seem to care about anyone else's opinion but her own.

Sometime later, the conversation in the classroom had turned to Harper's university work and the general day to day bores. The conversation had come to a pinnacle point in the discussion about the best place to get the weekly shop from, it was a close tie between the final two, when all of a sudden there was an abrupt knock followed by the door being flung open and in walked Detective Chief Inspector Barry Hughes quickly followed by Detective Inspector Jonathan Birch.

'Oh hello! Sorry we weren't expecting to see you, can we be of any assistance to you?' Frances greeted the two men with an element of surprise, she wasn't sure why, but Frances felt the need to be upstanding when in the presence of the two policemen.

'Hello ladies, sorry to interrupt. No, no help from either of you is necessary thank you,' Jonathan replied warmly. 'Just wrapping up a few loose ends.'

'Although whilst you are here you could help with one thing,' Barry stated as a matter of fact, his eyes were wondering over Caroline's old desk as his fingers gently combed through his straw-like moustache subconsciously. 'Has this desk been touched or has anything on the desk been moved since our team opened up the room again?'

'As far as I am aware no, I may have taken a pen out of the pot or used the scissors but apart from that no. Have you moved anything Harper?'

Harper shook her head in response. Frances' attention turned back to the detectives in front of her. Barry was flicking through images he had

produced from a folder which was being guarded by
Jonathan with every inch of his life.

'Are you sure there isn't anything we can do to help?'
Frances queried again, she felt uneasy being around
the authorities without knowing their intentions.

'No thank you,' Barry shut off the conversation as
he rearranged all the photographs handed them back
to Jonathan, who hastily stuffed them back into the
folder he was clutching before Barry stalked out of
the room as fast as his short legs could carry him.
Frances wondered how Hughes could have any air
of authority at that height.

The room fell silent, Harper was still sat at the table
filling out her paperwork keeping out the way and
Jonathan was stood gripping the folder looking lost,
he was unsure whether to follow Barry out of the
room or to stay put. Frances took this opportunity
to see what information she could drag out of him.

'So, Jonathan, how is the case going? Hope you
aren't being given too much of a hard time?'
Frances asked making a small nod towards the open
door when referencing to his short side kick.

'Oh, he isn't all that bad really, he's a completely different person once you get to know him,' Jonathan chuckled. Frances didn't believe any of it, but nodded and gave a small sigh in response, she was hoping not be around Hughes anymore to find out. 'He's only being uptight because we've been given new evidence which contradicts his theory,' Jonathan continued, obviously getting swept up in the thought of someone wanting to have a normal conversation with him that doesn't involve having orders barked at him.

But Frances heard exactly what she wanted to hear. The whole purpose of the conversation. New evidence. Frances clamped eyes on Jonathan, giving him an intent stare. She noticed that even Harper was showing intrigue in the conversation as she lifted her head in response to Jonathan's statement.

'New evidence?' Harper questioned.

'So, Hughes doesn't think it was a natural death now? Does he think it was murder?' Frances pushed on.

'Murder?' Harper gasped.

Frances didn't respond to Harper; she didn't have enough time to go into all that now. She had to push Jonathan further, she didn't know when she would get the opportunity to do this again.

'What new evidence?' Frances preserved.

'Uhh… I-I-I shouldn't have said anything. Pretend you didn't hear that,' Jonathan stuttered as he started waving his arms about.

'Jonathan. What new evidence?' Frances repeated.

'You know I'm not allowed to disclose any information with you,' He mumbled shuffling from one foot to the other.

'Well to be honest you already have,' Frances remarked. 'Come on Jonathan. I said to you after my interview that something didn't feel right, and it now seems the inspector feels the same!'

'I am not allowed to share any updates with potential suspects. The update isn't being shared with the general public yet!' Jonathan pleaded.

'I hardly know anyone! I'm a new face around this village. I'm not likely to be part of the Bertley Echo am I? I can reassure you this news will go no further,' She tried to reason. Frances completely forgot that Harper was here, but realistically someone like Harper hearing some confidential gossip isn't going to cause a catastrophe to the investigation, it's just Harper.

Jonathan gave a resigned sigh and perched against one of the tables, Frances got herself settled into the desk chair whilst Harper continued with her paperwork pretending not to listen.

'The new information came to life after the autopsy,' Jonathan began.

'So, it wasn't a natural death?' Frances repeated.

'It appears not. The autopsy shows damage to the lungs, which we are led to believe is the cause of death.'

'Damage to the lungs? How does that link to Caroline's death?' She pondered.

'It suggests that Caroline's death was caused by - '

'Inhalation,' Harper jumped in.

'Precisely,' Jonathan finished.

Frances looked puzzled. 'Inhalation? How is that possible? What could she have inhaled from the time I left her that could have killed her within an hour?'

'We don't know at the minute Miss, but we believe Caroline's death was caused due to inhalation. Our next step is to find out what she inhaled.'

Evidence Exposed...

Thursday evening, nine pm. The dark room was dimly lit by a laptop screen. The keys furiously tapping out accusations full of hate. The statement started:

'The dispute between Miss Caroline Macintosh and Miss Frances Garnham...'

The mouse hovered over the submit button on the screen.

Click.

The damage was done, and a sly smirk creeped across the shadowy face staring at the screen.

The plot was thickening for the police. But Frances had no idea she was about to be the main event.

***

Jonathan left the classroom after talking to Frances and Harper that Thursday afternoon and went in search of Barry Hughes, who he found stood by the main reception entrance looking rather impatient.

Barry clocked sight of Jonathan walking towards him and turned to him with his hands on his hips. 'Where have you been?' He demanded.

'Oh… um, I was just talking to Miss Garnham and Miss Craig-Lawson,' Jonathan responded trying to sound as casual as possible.

'Oh… I see,' Barry muttered and walked towards the police car.

Jonathan quickly followed, hoping that that would be the end of the conversation. Unfortunately for him it wasn't.

Barry clicked his seat belt closed, turned on the car engine and made a swift exit out of the school car park and sped along the country roads. He then turned his attention back to interrogating Jonathan. 'I hope you weren't discussing new police knowledge with her,' he spat, emphasising 'her'.

Jonathan gulped. 'No of course not. That's against all protocol,' Jonathan lied, hoping that Barry was focusing on the road and not on Jonathan's readable face.

Barry nodded. 'Good, I don't trust Miss Garnham.'

'With all due respect Sir, you don't trust many people,' Jonathan remarked.

Barry's head snapped round to face Jonathan with a glare. 'Particularly when she is the main suspect in an investigation.'

Jonathan stopped frozen in his seat. 'Main suspect? What makes Miss Garnham the main suspect?'

'Oh, come off it Birch. Do you not think it's strange that a primary school has had no police involvement, all of a sudden there's an unexplained death the morning after a new arrival enters the school. And that new arrival happens to be the new teaching assistant of the deceased!'

'That maybe, but that doesn't necessarily mean anything-' Jonathan started.

'See this is why you will never progress to my level Jonathan,' Barry stated smugly. 'Did you not notice that in the interview with Miss Garnham it became clear that her and Miss Macintosh didn't see eye to eye. She said that herself! And that all happened on the first day of them meeting, twenty-four hours before Caroline's death!'

'I understand that Sir,' Jonathan agreed before contradicting him. 'But lots of the staff there didn't see eye to eye with the deceased. Max said that Caroline irritated him. Amanda clashed with Caroline frequently,' he justified.

'I'm telling you Birch. Frances Garnham had something to do with Caroline's death.'

Jonathan fell silent and turned his head to face the window. He had the feeling that he wasn't going to win this argument, no matter how much counter evidence he had. Once Barry had an idea about something, it was the only right answer. The pair drove the rest of the way back to the police station in silence.

***

Jonathan was relieved that Friday had finally arrived. The week had definitely seemed longer when constantly being in the company of Barry Hughes so he will be glad to have two days away from him.

He had just managed to settle down into his chair to trawl through lots of paperwork and written statements when the door suddenly burst open, reverberating off the filing cabinet nearby. Barry Hughes strolled in through the doorway in a cocky manner wearing a conceited grin on his face waving a piece of paper at Jonathan.

'What did I say? What did I say Birch?' Barry tossed the piece of paper in Jonathan's direction.

Jonathan picked up the paper and upon seeing the information internally groaned. 'Oh, what have you done?' He thought. 'What have you gotten yourself into?'

'Did I not say she had something to do with all this?' Barry bragged stalking towards the door. 'Come on Birch, this is the evidence we need. Let's go, we don't have a moment to lose.'

Jonathan sighed and slowly got up from his chair grabbing his jacket as he shuffled across the room. He was dreading doing what he was about to do. All he could heard was Barry's bellowing voice traveling throughout the police station.

'Come on! We've got our evidence, let's see what she makes of this. Let's bring her in.'

***

The car ride to the school was long and torturous for Jonathan. He knew that Frances wasn't responsible for what happened to Caroline, but he couldn't get Barry to see that. His mind was charged with questions.

If Frances didn't do this, then why would someone provide the police with this evidence?

Who did send this anonymous information to the police?

Why didn't Frances tell them about this when they first spoke to her?

Was it because she did have something to do with this?

'No that's ridiculous Jonathan. Who tries to investigate a murder when they have committed it?' He scolded himself.

However, many times he tried to rack his brains for reasonable explanations, Jonathan never came to an answer. Instead, the car slowly pulled up to the school and Barry reversed into the nearest parking space.

For the first time in his job Jonathan felt sick with guilt and regret as he unbuckled his seatbelt and rolled out of the passenger side of the car. He knew this was wrong. Things didn't add up, nothing made sense. But Jonathan had no choice but to follow Detective Hughes through the main reception down the never-ending corridor towards the year one classroom door. The Inspector briskly knocked on the door waiting for a response from someone inside. Jonathan had his fingers crossed inside his jacket pocket, hoping that no one answered so that they would have to leave.

Unfortunately, the classroom door was pulled open a few minutes later and the two police officers were greeted by a confused Harper. 'Oh, good afternoon detectives, can I help you?' She asked, sceptical of the officer's intentions.

'Good morning, Miss Craig-Lawson do you happen to know the whereabouts of Miss Garnham?'

Harper blinked looking surprised. 'Frances? She was here earlier on this morning, but I believe she has gone to speak to one of the other teachers.'

'I see, do you mind if we come inside and wait for her please. We need her... assistance in our investigation.' Barry queried.

'Oh well y-yes of course, I am sure she won't be much longer,' Harper opened the door further and stepped aside, inviting the policemen into the classroom.

Barry nodded a thank you to Harper and made a bee line to stand by the teacher's desk.

Jonathon hoped for Frances' sake that she wouldn't return to the classroom for a while.

Suspects Eliminated and Under Accusations…

At last, the end of what had seemed to be a very long week was finally in sight. Not that Frances was very focussed on that, her head was still racing with thoughts about Caroline's mysterious death. Luckily for her, Frances was able to unload and share her continuous thoughts with Harper, who was more than happy to listen whilst printing and trimming paperwork.

'I still can't get my head around it, there must be some kind of mistake. Surely, she can't have died from inhaling something, I would have smelt it. And how would someone have managed it without being seen?' Frances puzzled as she was shuffling papers around.

'Surely the main question is why would someone want to cause Caroline harm, that would bring you one step closer to how it was done?' Harper suggested.

'As much as that is a good theory to work on, it seems like most people if not everyone had some reason to hate Caroline so that hasn't narrowed down my options,' Frances huffed, pausing to chew on the end of her pen.

'Okay so let's look at it from a different angle. Where was everyone in the hour before Caroline was discovered? That way anyone you were with couldn't have done it! That will narrow down your list a bit.'

'Good idea!' Frances placed her pen down and leant forward in her chair, becoming fully invested to the point of creating a plan of the school and placing everyone in the rooms where they were when the crime would have taken place, but then that might be a sign for her to stop playing *Cluedo* for a while.

'So, who were you with that morning?' Probed Harper.

'I met up with Dylan, Alice and Grace in the staffroom, we got our drinks and headed straight to the hall for the meeting.'

'Okay so it can't have been any of them. Did you see anyone else?'

'Mm... Oh I met Ian and Grant in the staffroom, but that was very brief,' Frances recalled.

'Okay so if nobody else saw them that morning then they still had time to set up the scene and kill Caroline,' Harper deliberated.

Frances was impressed, Harper had a clear layout of who could have committed the crime, something Frances was struggling to do. Perhaps involving Harper in her little investigation wasn't such a bad idea after all.

'So, who else can we rule out?' Harper continued.

'Well, we can obviously rule you out because you hadn't arrived yet, and you discovered Caroline so you definitely couldn't have done it,' Frances stated making a pointed gesture towards Harper.

'So, we are left with Adeline, Charlotte, Amanda, Max, Grant, Ian, Agatha, Lennox and Mildred.'

The room then became full of silent thoughts as Frances and Harper began running through their detective theories to themselves. Looking at the remaining suspects, Frances recalled on how Grant and Max were acting in the staffroom after Caroline's body had been discovered. They were huddled in the corner chatting amongst themselves whilst dubiously glancing at everyone else in the room. And knowing that they were both still suspects made her more suspicious.

'I don't see why Ian would have done it,' Frances voiced her thoughts, breaking the silence.

'What makes you think that?'

Frances nestled into her chair as she laid out her reasonings. 'Well, he always had similar teaching views to Caroline. I know they were always competing to win brain box of the year, but I really don't think he had enough of a motive to kill her.'

'That makes sense, but he still doesn't have a secure alibi for that morning,' Harper pointed out.

Frances thought about it for a moment, casting her mind back to the first time she met Ian. Suddenly she had a light bulb moment, snapping her fingers which startled Harper. 'He can't have done it, he can't have!' Frances gasped.

'How do you know?'

'Because he went nowhere near Caroline's classroom! As Ian was leaving the staffroom, he turned right heading towards the hall, the opposite way to Caroline's classroom!'

'Are you sure?'

'A hundred percent I watched him leave! And after Ian left, we followed shortly after, and Ian was there when we made it to the hall. It can't have been Ian,' Frances responded confidently.

'Well in that case we can rule Ian out. Only seven suspects to go.'

***

Frances knocked on the year six classroom door and waited for an invitation to come in. She didn't really want to have this conversation, but she had to ask someone, she had to know. Instead, the door swung open, and Frances was met with a very perplexed Charlotte.

'Oh… hello, sorry it's-'

'Frances,' She jumped in. 'It's okay, no worries. It hasn't really been a getting acquainted kind of situation,' Frances gave an awkward chuckle, she guessed Charlotte wasn't really one for jokes as she responded with a soft smile.

'Sorry can I help you with something?' Charlotte quietly asked.

'Oh, right yes,' Frances responded. 'Could I ask you a question?'

'Um…' Charlotte glanced at her watch.

'I will be five minutes, I promise. I know you have a lot to be getting on with, but it's really important,' Frances was practically begging.

Charlotte sighed and slowly nodded as she opened the classroom door. 'Okay, go for it.'

Frances gave Charlotte a smile of gratitude and scurried into the classroom. Charlotte closed the door and made her way back to her desk chair.

'So, what is so important?' Charlotte wasn't messing around.

'Okay so I won't beat around the bush, I will just come straight out with it,' Frances began, she was stalling, and she knew she was but there was absolutely no way of asking this without offending Charlotte and she didn't want to do that. But she had no choice, and she knew that too. Frances needed to know. Charlotte was beginning to look more clueless as time went on. 'Where were you the morning Caroline died?' Frances blurted.

Charlotte looked stunned. 'I'm sorry. What did you just say?'

'W-w-where were you... the morning Caroline died?' Frances repeated.

Charlotte paused. 'Why do you want to know?' She asked cautiously.

'Well… you see, I was thinking about it all… and something didn't seem right. S-so I thought-'

'What. You thought I had something to do with it?' Charlotte struck back.

'No! No not at all!' Frances tried to reassure.

'So why are you asking me this?'

'Because!' Frances stopped and took a deep breathe. 'Because this whole situation seems odd to me. Are you telling me that you don't think it's strange that one minute Caroline is completely fine and then is found the following morning… dead?'

Charlotte pondered for a minute. 'I can see what you are saying. You're right it was a shock, completely unexpected. So, what have my whereabouts got to do with anything?'

'Don't get me wrong, I don't think any of the staff had anything to do with this. But if I can work out where everyone was before Caroline was found then we can look at who was more likely to have seen Caroline, they might have seen or heard something that might lead to what actually happened.'

'Surely that's a job for the police?' Charlotte put forward.

'The inspector was adamant it was a death of natural causes,' Frances shrugged.

'Ah I see,' Charlotte nodded slowly. 'Well, if you must know, I was on the hall helping Adeline set up the laptop for the staff meeting that morning. Amanda was meant to be doing it, but she was probably in her own little bubble faffing, so Adeline asked me. And if you don't believe me, you can ask Agatha she was there setting up the tables.'

'So that rules out Adeline and Agatha too,' Frances mumbled, obviously not quiet enough though.

'Oh, you can't be serious, you seriously didn't think Adeline had something to do with it. It would completely ruin her career!' Charlotte cried in disbelief.

'No, I know she wouldn't do anything. Adeline doesn't have a bad bone in her body. But Adeline had no alibi for that morning, but now the three of you were together and nowhere near the classroom then you can't have seen or heard anything.'

'That makes sense. Glad to have cleared that up. I know I said Caroline should have been taken down a peg or two, but I wouldn't have acted on it; apart from the occasional clash I hardly spoke to her anyway! And yes, Caroline and Adeline had friction between them, but they were always civil to each other nothing would have come of it,' Charlotte justified.

'I know,' Frances sighed. 'I personally don't see how anyone here would have done it.' The pair didn't talk for a while. Suddenly Frances remembered that she promised to keep this conversation short, so she wasn't keeping Charlotte from her work. She slowly moved across the room. 'Anyway, I've kept you for long enough I will let you get on. Thank you for answering that, I didn't mean to cause any offence.'

'Don't worry about it,' Charlotte waved her off before quickly turning back. 'But Frances, if you are going to tread these waters and really find out what happened then please be careful. If someone did hurt Caroline, then they may think about trying to keep you quiet.'

'I will, thank you Charlotte,' Frances gave her a grateful smile, an awkward wave and left the room quietly closing the door behind her.

On her way back to the classroom, Frances was raking her brains over the left-over suspects:

Amanda.   Max.   Grant.   Lennox and Mildred.

She couldn't understand how any of these people would want to get rid of Caroline. But then her thoughts went back to something Charlotte warned her about:

'If someone did hurt Caroline then they may think twice about trying to keep you quiet.'

Does this mean Charlotte was suspicious of someone? They? Could there be more than one person involved? Frances knew that she would have to be wary of who she spoke to about this. She was starting to lose trust in her colleagues.

Her thoughts would have to wait till later, her eyes were caught by a photo on the wall. It was an old whole school photo. Frances went to take a closer look. The photo was taken years ago, it was labelled two thousand and six. She thought she recognised some of the teachers in the picture and of course Lennox and Mildred. All of a sudden Frances was drawn to one particular child, in the third row up eight in from the left. It was strange she had never been in this village, but she thought she knew this child, as if she had seen them before but she couldn't work out why. Frances was so entranced by this discovery that she didn't hear Mildred walking towards her.

'You alright Frances?'

Frances leapt into the air. 'Oh Mildred! You frightened the life out of me!' Frances gasped placing a hand on her frantically beating heart.

'Sorry lovely, you seemed to be in your own little world,' Mildred apologised.

'I must have been,' Frances sighed calming herself down before turning her attention back to the photograph. 'I was just looking at this. Is that you and Lennox on the far right?'

'Oh yes! This was a lovely year. This was one of the first years Lennox and I worked here. And there's Adeline, she had only been teaching a couple of years back then.'

'This was before she became a headteacher?' Frances questioned. If Mildred was willing to delve into the school's past, then Frances might as well find out as much as she can. She might even find out from Mildred who the mysterious child was.

'Oh yeah, Adeline started out just like the rest of us you know,' Mildred chuckled. 'Oh, look there's Grace. And Ian, they all look so young! Oh, and there's... Caroline.' Mildred gave a small sad smile. Frances followed to where Mildred was looking, sure enough there was a younger Caroline with the same look of pride about her, but she seemed to be smiling. Maybe Caroline hadn't always been so reserved and strict.

Frances tried to change the subject; she hated seeing Mildred upset. 'Who's that?' She asked pointing to the child, third row up eight in from the left.

Mildred snapped out from her trip down memory lane and turned her attention back to the photo. Her face suddenly changed; she looked puzzled. 'Do you know I have absolutely no idea,' Mildred's face was worrying to Frances.

'You alright Mildred?'

'Oh yes, I'm alright. I just know that face. I have definitely seen them before. I just can't for the life of me think of who they are,' Mildred chuckled.

Frances could understand why Mildred would know them, it was alarming to Frances that she had the same feeling as Mildred, especially when Frances had never stepped foot in this village before.

Once Frances had finally managed to escape from what could have turned into an hour-long conversation with Mildred, she raced back to the classroom. She wanted to share her findings from

Charlotte with Harper. Harper might also be able to find out who the child in the photo was for Frances, she might be able to find the school records online.

Frances flung the door open, rambling before she had seen who was in there waiting for her. 'Okay so update,' Frances started as she was shutting the door. 'Charlotte and Agatha were setting up in the main hall with Adeline so it can't have been any of those three, which means - Oh!' Frances stopped dead in her tracks as she was met by the sight of the two detectives in front of her. Harper looked alarmed. 'Hello gentlemen, lovely day we are having,' Frances tried to lighten what was becoming an awkward mood; it didn't work.

'Hello Miss Garnham,' Barry greeted her coldly.

Frances didn't feel like this was the time to correct him that he could call her Frances because she hated Miss Garnham, so she would let it slide this time.

'We would like you to accompany us to the station please.'

Harper's head snapped around to look at Frances as Frances' blood ran cold.

This can't be happening.

'Can I ask why?' Frances enquired, trying to remain cool.

'It's just to answer some questions,' Jonathan tried reassuring her.

'Well, is the station really necessary? I am quite happy to answer your questions here, we can go into the staffroom or Adeline would be more than happy to make the office available to us?' Frances was practically pleading with the officers.

'Miss Garnham allow me to put it this way. You can either accompany us to the station or I will have no choice but to arrest you for perverting the course of justice,' Barry Hughes gave it the best way he knew how, straight to the point.

Frances felt like she was in a nightmare, and she had no way of escaping. Frances had no choice. She quickly nodded her head, collected her belongings which she threw and locked away in her car and followed the officers to their police car.

Her palms were sweating.

Her heart was racing.

But there was nothing Frances could do.

Frances Garnham was sat in the back of the police car wondering how she got there.

Intense Interrogation and A Helping Hand…

The interview room was cold, grey and dark. The only essence of light that segmented the never-ending walls was from the large singular window. Inside the room was a small wooden table surrounded by four plastic chairs, which Frances knew were uncomfortable because she was sat on one of them. The officers had dropped Frances off here and left her to go and get paperwork.

Just as Frances was worrying that they had forgotten about her, the door flew open and in walked Barry with all the authority a man of his demeanour could pull off, followed by Jonathan who gave Frances an apologetic look as he took his seat diagonally across from her. Barry however showed no remorse, holding Frances' gaze as he reached across and pressed record on the small tape machine that was to the right of the table.

The room was filled with the sound of an ear-piercing bleep. The noise seemed to last for what felt like hours, however long it did last for it was not enough time for Frances to try and arrange her racing thoughts:

Why has she been brought here?

Did they think she was responsible?

How was she going to get out of this one?

At last, the beeping finally stopped, and it was the moment Detective Barry Hughes had done all this training for. 'Police interview carried out by Detective Chief Inspector Barry Hughes and Detective Inspector Jonathan Birch. Interviewing Miss Frances Garnham, interview taking place Friday at four thirty pm. The purpose of the interview is to gain further information with regard to the death of Miss Caroline Macintosh. Miss Garnham this interview is being recorded; you may choose to leave at any time. You don't have to say anything but anything you do say may be used as evidence and you have the right to legal representation. Is that all clear Miss Garnham and do you require legal representation?'

Frances paused for a moment, preparing herself for the inevitable bombardment of questions she was about to face, looked Barry in the eye and responded as calmly as she could manage. 'That won't be necessary thank you.'

Barry nodded, opened the folder and pulled out a piece of paperwork. 'Miss Garnham when we last spoke you said that yourself and Caroline didn't see eye-to-eye, can you tell us more about that?'

'Well as I said to you when we last spoke, Caroline and I shared different views in regard to the teaching profession.'

'Can you expand on that please Miss,' Jonathan interjected.

'Um... of course. Caroline's ideas of teaching were very... old school. As I had recently graduated from my teaching degree, my teaching views were more recent and to some people new. That is in no way an insult to Caroline, I was working in her classroom, so I was happy to work by Caroline's way.'

Barry was not wasting any time. 'Why didn't you tell us about the fall out you and Caroline had the day before Caroline's death?'

Frances was flummoxed. 'E-e-e-excuse me? Falling out? Who told you about that?'

'Unfortunately, we are not at liberty to disclose any names,' Jonathan murmured.

'But you don't understand it wasn't an argument it was just a misunderstanding,' Frances fumbled.

'We will be the judge of that Miss,' Barry jumped in.

Frances gave Barry a horrified stare, she couldn't believe what was happening, they were treating her like a criminal... a murderer. She was even more determined to prove Barry Hughes wrong. She was innocent.

'I can assure you there was no argument between myself and Caroline. I simply asked Caroline which group of children she wanted me to work with when the children came into school. Caroline didn't take it very well, so she made it clear that I was to go by her way in the classroom, that was all,' Frances stated confidently.

'So you didn't question her teaching and make her feel threatened?' Barry questioned.

'What, no I-' Frances stumbled.

'So, she didn't make it very clear to you that you are just a teaching assistant and that you use foolish methods?' He continued.

'She said that yes, but-'

'And did she not threaten to have you removed from the classroom if you were not up to her standard?' Barry stared Frances down, he wasn't going to give Frances any reason to think she could get out of this easily, and she knew this.

'Who's been telling you this?' Frances demanded.

Barry leaned back in his seat with a smirk on his face, he knew he was getting to her. 'You trained as a teacher, but you are working as a teaching assistant, why is that?'

Frances sighed. 'I haven't been able to get a teaching job yet, so when I saw the teaching assistant role, I thought I would try that as I am still getting experience in the teaching profession, which will help me to get a teaching job in the future.'

'Well, you don't have to worry about that now do you?' Barry retorted.

Frances looked confused. 'Excuse me? I don't quite follow.'

'Well now you have a teaching job, you're taking over from Caroline.'

'Oh, for heaven's sake,' Frances rolled her eyes. 'I did not kill Caroline!'

'It's worked out very well for you, you've got to admit,' Barry pushed on.

'Anyone at that school could have killed Caroline, I don't know if you are aware because you are too fixated on persecuting me, but Caroline didn't have many raving reviews from the staff,' Frances bit back.

'So, you're saying you didn't decide you could do a better job than Caroline and thought you could get rid of her and take her place,' Barry persisted.

'No! Why would I kill somebody I had only met twenty-four hours ago? You can keep trying to push this point, but I am telling you the truth. I did not kill Caroline,' Frances snapped back.

The room fell silent. Frances was hoping that this was going to be the end of the grilling. Unfortunately, Barry Hughes had one more question in store. 'Where were you the morning of Caroline's death?'

'I've already told you all of this!' Frances exasperated quietly.

'Please just clarify your whereabouts for that morning Miss,' Jonathan politely asked. He seemed to finally find his voice after the row between Barry and Frances.

Frances leant back in her plastic chair and raked a hand through her hair. 'I arrived at eight in the morning. I saw Caroline when I arrived in the classroom to drop off my bags off and had a brief conversation with her. At quarter-past eight I headed to the staffroom, whilst in there I met Alice McKenzie, Dylan Walker and Grace Taylor, we stayed in the staffroom chatting and making a drink. We then headed to the hall for the staff meeting at quarter-to nine. After that I was in the hall with everyone else and that's where I was when Harper came in to tell us about Caroline.'

'And you didn't see anyone else?' Jonathan asked.

'Only Grant Kennedy and Ian Marshall, but that was briefly in the staffroom.'

'Well thank you Miss Garnham. We will be back momentarily. Interview terminated at five fifteen,' Barry promptly stopped the tape recording, collected his paperwork into the folder and marched towards the door in one swift movement, leaving Jonathan stumbling behind. The only farewell Frances received was a sympathetic smile from Jonathan as he closed the door behind him.

The only thing Frances could manage was to put her head in her hands. She felt defeated and tired, she had done all she could now she just had to hope that the detectives saw that she was innocent. There was one thing Frances couldn't get her head around. Who told the police that her and Caroline had had an argument? Even though the officers couldn't tell her who said it, she could narrow it down to being someone at the school.

Who would want to falsely accuse Frances?

She was sure she hadn't made any enemies.

Well one thing was for certain, someone had framed her for a crime she did not commit, and she needed to find out who it was.

A little while later the door opened again and Barry Hughes walked in, looking more annoyed compared to the smug look he left with earlier.

'Right Miss Garnham, we are releasing you under investigation. You are free to go.'

Frances breathed a sigh of relief as she rose from the plastic chair. She was grateful to be leaving as the chair was so uncomfortable, she was beginning to go numb from the waist down.

'Thank you. Would someone be able to call me a taxi back to the school please.'

'There's no need Miss, I will drop you off there,' Jonathan jumped in.

'Oh, are you sure? I don't want to put you out.'

'No, it's not a problem at all, it's on my way home anyway,' he reassured her.

Frances gave Jonathan a smile. 'Thank you, I appreciate that.'

Jonathan motioned for Frances to leave the room first, which she did without a second thought. Only as she entered the corridor did she hear Jonathan address his boss with a simple goodbye.

***

Frances was racking her brains to think of a conversation starter. She didn't want this to be an awkward car ride, she liked Jonathan and didn't have anything against him. It wasn't his fault his boss had a bee in his bonnet against her and was determined to cast her as the criminal. 'So, do you live far from the school then?' She started out.

'Er, yes. Just over there,' Jonathan pointed behind the two front car seats towards the back of the car.

Frances looked behind her confused. 'But... that's in the other direction.'

'I know. About twenty minutes in the other direction to be exact,' Jonathan gave Frances a shrug.

'I don't understand, why are you doing this then? Surely someone else could have dropped me off?'

'They could have, but I wanted to talk to you about something,' came the blunt response.

'Sounds ominous,' Frances chuckled to which Jonathan joined in. 'Then why didn't you say anything back at the station?'

'Because in all honesty I could lose my job sharing this with you,' Jonathan admitted.

Frances looked stunned. 'Wow, it really must be serious then! I don't want to put your job in jeopardy.'

'Well, I'm glad to hear that because it means this conversation can go no further.'

'My lips are sealed,' Frances closed her lips like pulling a zip shut. The pair shared a laugh before Jonathan became serious again.

'I don't think you had anything to do with Caroline's death. I think the closest involvement you have with all this is that you are doing your own investigation to find out who did it, which I think you need to be careful with-'

'Wait, how did you know I am investigating all this?' Frances chimed in, giving a dramatically offended look.

'Because you started telling Miss Craig-Lawson about your findings earlier on today when we met you in the classroom,' Jonathan answered, giving Frances an '*I told you so*' look.

'Wow you are good at what you do,' Frances remarked. 'Well, you've got me there, you might as well arrest me now.' Frances put her wrists together ready to go into handcuffs.

Jonathan laughed and shook his head. 'That won't be necessary. But I do think you need to be careful because I think someone is trying to frame you for Caroline's death. So be careful with what information you share and with whom. Consider yourself told off,' Jonathan pointed a finger at Frances; she slapped her wrist as a response.

'Do you think the person setting me up is the same person who told you about the disagreement between myself and Caroline?' Frances continued.

'Could be yes, which is why you need to be careful it's obviously someone you are close to.'

'Who told you about that by the way?' Frances slipped into the conversation.

Jonathan rolled his eyes and shook his head. 'You know I can't tell you that.'

'Not even a little clue?' Frances teased.

'No, I am already risking my job for you!' Jonathan laughed.

'And for that I am honoured,' Frances smiled placing her hand over the top of her heart.

'Anyway, I couldn't tell you who it was because the information was sent to us by an anonymous email,' Jonathan explained.

'Now that is odd,' Frances pondered for a moment before trying again. 'You couldn't tell me the email address it was sent from then?' Frances gave Jonathan a cheeky smile.

He gave her a raised eyebrow, and then rolled his eyes as he chuckled. 'I will think about it. But I don't see how that knowledge will be of any help to you though.'

'I don't know but I would appreciate it if you could send it to me somehow.'

At this point Jonathan pulled up outside the school car park. Frances was a little disappointed the car ride was over; it was nice being able to discuss things with someone she knew she could trust. And it was a bonus, a reassurance to know that someone believed her and was on her side.

'Well thank you for the lift back and the heart-to-heart chat, we should do that again!' Frances giggled.

'Yeah, we should,' Jonathan chuckled. 'And don't worry about the lift, I needed to find time to warn you. Be careful with who you talk to okay?'

'I will do, *Brownies* promise,' Frances held up the *Brownies* salute. She was just about to get out the car when Jonathan stopped her.

'Oh! Before you go, I wanted to share something with you.'

Frances looked back at Jonathan puzzled.

'We know what substance was used to kill Caroline.'

Frances gasped and turned round in her seat, so she was fully facing Jonathan. 'Will you get into trouble for telling me this as well?' Frances said with a concerned look.

'I will but I thought you might need to know for your investigation.'

'Ah very true,' Frances nodded.

'Exactly,' Jonathan agreed. 'Well drum roll please. Caroline Macintosh was murdered with hydrochloric acid.'

'Wow! Really? I wasn't expecting that.'

'Well, it does make sense, doesn't take an awful lot to become dangerous. Five millilitres is all that's needed.'

'Blimey, how do you know it's definitely that?' Frances asked.

'The coroner said all the signs lead to it being hydrochloric acid. Swelling of the throat leading to suffocation, corrosive burning on the lungs and laryngeal burning. It all adds up,' Jonathan explained.

'Yeah... I suppose it does,' Frances went into a daze.

'Well, I best be getting off then, let you get home as you've had quite a day today,' Jonathan broke into her thoughts.

'Yes, thanks again for the lift and the new information. I really appreciate it,' Frances replied giving an appreciative smile.

'Anytime, and Frances please be careful,' Jonathan called as she stepped out the car.

'I will,' Frances shut the car door gave Jonathan a wave and headed towards her car.

After watching Jonathan drive away, Frances unlocked her car, settled herself into the driver's seat and threw her head against the headrest with the longest sigh. Knowing there's a cup of tea waiting for her at home as her motivation, Frances started the car headed for the car park entrance and made a beeline for the open country roads.

Cross-Examinations Continues...

Monday morning came around too fast and before she knew it, Frances was back in the classroom. Although the room was full of a static feeling, a feeling of anticipation. It was the new start of the term after all the altercations that had happened the previous week, so the children would be returning to the school today. Despite preparing all the paperwork, reading through lesson plan multiple times last night and receiving a motivational pep talk from Adeline this morning as she clocked in, Frances did not feel prepared. So, she felt a slight reassurance to know she wasn't facing today alone and has a companion in Harper to lean on for support. It's just a shame that her current choice of conversation wasn't a better distraction.

'So, what did the detectives want to talk to you about yesterday?'

''Oh, they just wanted to bombard me with a load of questions really. A complete waste of time in all honesty,' Frances hoped she sounded more relaxed about it all than how she actually felt. Yesterday's encounter really shook her.

'Oh, completely typical of the police then,' Harper chuckled. Frances smiled and rolled her eyes exaggeratively. 'Anyway, you were trying to tell me something yesterday as you came back into the classroom, but you didn't get to finish as the police were here,' Harper continued.

'Oh yes! So, I spoke to Charlotte, and she was helping Adeline and Agatha setting up the hall for the staff meeting. So, none of them could have gone to see Caroline,' Frances updated.

'Well at least that reduces the list of suspects. We're getting quite good at this!' Harper exclaimed clapping her hands gleefully.

'Indeed,' Frances nodded and chuckled. 'And as a bonus, I managed to find out what Caroline inhaled which killed her.'

'Really? How on earth did you manage that?' Harper looked gobsmacked.

'I have my ways,' Frances told her smugly tapping the side of her nose. She remembered the conversation she had with Jonathan last night and didn't want to drop him in it after he had gone to all that trouble to tell her. She also remembered how he urged her to be careful, but knowing it was only going to Harper she knew there wouldn't be any issues.

'Alright then clever clogs, what was it?' Harper huffed jokingly.

'Hydrochloric acid.' Frances proudly announced. Harper was too stunned to speak. 'I know, so call me a genius but that means whoever did this must be good with their periodic table,' Frances pointed out.

'Ah well in that case our suspect list just got smaller!" Harper exclaimed.

Frances tilted her head to one side looking bewildered. 'How so? Surely everyone knows where the acids are kept? They are in the cleaning cupboard, even I know that!' Having said this, Frances only knew where the cleaning cupboard was because it was known as the crying cupboard where most of the staff went to have a breakdown.

'Well yeah but not everyone knows all about them. Whereas Lennox and Mildred regularly use hydrochloric acid when cleaning,' Harper justified.

'Right,' Frances acknowledged.

'Plus, Mildred and Lennox often complained about Caroline. They could have easily set up the crime that morning when they came in to start cleaning,' Harper reasoned.

'But how would have they have done it?' Frances pondered.

'I don't know! They could have covered the whiteboard in the stuff or the desk, or even have left an open bottle of the stuff under the table! Or all else fails could have soaked a cloth in the stuff and smothered her with it!' Harper cried.

Frances raised a single eyebrow at her and gave a small chuckle. 'That's a bit excessive don't you think?'

'Well yeah of course it is, but they could have done it in multiple ways that we don't know about. Just because we don't know how they did it doesn't mean that we can rule them out.' Harper conveyed exasperatedly.

Frances slowly nodded as she considered Harper's reasons. She could see why Harper thought of the Campbells as possible suspects, they didn't like Caroline or how she was with the children. But Frances remembered the chat she had with Mildred the other day, and the look of melancholy on Mildred's face as she saw the old whole school photo with Caroline. Despite the hate they shared, Frances was positive that neither Lennox nor Mildred were capable of killing Caroline. At least she hoped she was right.

'Or if not them,' Harper broke into the silence. 'It could be Max.'

Frances snapped out of her thoughts at the sound of another name. 'Max? How come?'

'Well, you've probably guessed that he wasn't a fan of Caroline. But before he got a job here, he worked at a secondary school!'

'No way!' Frances gasped.

'I know right! Anyway, the best bit is that when he worked at the secondary school, he was a teacher of science! So when he got the job here, they made him science subject lead and he is in charge of restocking or ordering new equipment for science lessons. I mean come on surely that's not a coincidence.'

Frances couldn't believe it. All the answers she needed had to come to her all at once, she was dumbstruck. 'That makes so much sense,' Frances whispered. 'He would know all about the side effects of hydrochloric acid.'

'And we don't have any knowledge of his whereabouts for that morning,' Harper stated as a matter of fact.

'Which means nobody saw him that morning, and his classroom is next door to Caroline's, so he could have easily gone there and set up the crime,' Frances continued. Harper nodded slowly, taking in all the new knowledge.

Before they could discuss it anymore, the noise of children in the playground interrupted them. It was quarter-to nine, the school day would be starting soon.

'Right, we'll have to carry on this discussion later,' Frances quickly cleared up the leftover paperwork. 'Let's muddle through and see how today goes.'

'We'll be fine! We're the dream team,' Harper called positively, offering Frances a high five as she did so.

Frances chuckled, she was grateful to have people at the school who trusted her and knew of her innocence. 'In that case, are you ready Miss Craig-Lawson?'

'I'm ready if you're ready Miss Garnham?'

***

The school day had gone well overall, Frances and Harper managed to make it through the day together. The children were welcoming to Frances, the whole atmosphere gave off no inkling that this time a week ago all chaos was about to unfold, and Caroline would be found dead 24 hours later. But by three-thirty Frances was frazzled, keeping up the persona of a welcoming teacher all the while picking her way through the thoughts chasing around her mind took an awful lot of work. In spite of this, however much Frances wanted to go home and sleep the day off, she knew there was something she needed to do first.

She'd sent Harper home already; she didn't want her to be dragged into this conversation. She knocked on the door of the year two classroom, knots were forming in her stomach. This is the moment she could uncover everything.

The door swinging open startled Frances as she locked eyes on a smiling Max. 'Frances, hi! How did today go?' He chirped.

'Hi, um… yeah it was fine thanks. Yeah, it went really well,' Frances stammered.

Max looked concerned. 'You okay? Do you want to come in and have a sit down?'

'Huh? Oh yeah, I am fine really. Just tired,' Frances answered. Max nodded, not looking very convinced. Seeing as Max had given her the perfect incentive, Frances took it. 'But could I come in? There is something I wanted to talk to you about,' Frances bravely whispered, glancing around as she spoke to check for any prying ears.

Max copied Frances and started glancing around, not entirely sure what he was looking for, and then stepped aside to allow Frances to walk through. Max closed the door behind him as Frances rested against the edge of one of the tables. 'Are you sure you're alright? I know that the first day can be tiring and overwhelming, but is something worrying you?' He reiterated as he sat back at his desk.

'I'm fine honestly. Although yeah you can say that again, I am exhausted,' Frances chuckled; Max gave her a soft smile in response. 'But there is something that doesn't sit right with me. It's about Caroline's death.'

Max's face dropped, he quickly turned to focus on sorting out the pens in the pencil pot on his desk, keeping his gaze away from Frances. 'Right... I don't see why you are worrying about that Frances; I am sure the police are on the case if you'll pardon the pun,' he briefly turned to face Frances to see if she had got the joke. But when she didn't smile or laugh in response, his gaze quickly reverted to the pencil pot before he continued. 'Well, what's worrying you?'

'Okay, so I heard that you were a science teacher in a secondary school before you came here,' Frances started, not entirely sure where to look.

'I don't see how that had anything to do with Caroline's death. But uh yeah I was, I discovered I preferred teaching children that didn't tower above me or didn't talk back!' Max chuckled but Frances didn't smile.

'I see,' she paused. 'So, you would know the side effects of inhaling something like hydrochloric acid?'

Max grew concerned again. 'Erm, y-yes, I suppose I do yeah. Why do you ask?'

'So, knowing that, where would you put it in a room if you were going to use it to hurt someone?' Frances carried on, pushing through the conversation.

The room went uncomfortably quiet, Frances didn't dare to try and make eye contact with Max so instead she stared at the floor fidgeting with her hands.

'Frances, why are you asking me this?' Max quizzed her again. She couldn't bring herself to answer, so she just sat there. It suddenly seemed to dawn on him. 'You don't think I had something to do with it, do you?' He asked quietly.

'Oh, I don't know! I don't know what to think anymore,' she groaned, throwing her head into her hands.

Max sighed. 'What makes you think I would want to do something like that?'

'Oh, come off it Max, you wished me good luck when you first met me and found out I was going to be in Caroline's class! You hated her!' Frances cried.

'I think hate is slightly exaggerative. Hate is a very strong word,' Max corrected.

'You said the best thing to happen would be if the school got rid of Caroline and replaced her. I think hate describes it perfectly,' Frances retorted bitterly.

'Yeah okay, valid point. But may I remind you that everyone hated her, it wasn't like a personal vendetta I had against her!' Max fought back.

'But you know where the acids are kept, you had easy access to them and knew all about them. It would have been so easy for you to plan all of this and get away with it without anyone batting an eyelid-'

'Okay, I'm gonna stop you there,' Max interrupted, holding a hand up making Frances stop mid-sentence. 'First of all, that cupboard is open to everyone so anyone can access the chemicals in there. And secondly anyone in this school could research into hydrochloric acid or could ask me about the dangers and say it was for a risk assessment. Both Charlotte and Harper asked me about it a while back! So again, anyone could have done this and be framing me for it.' Max justified.

'I just don't know what to believe anymore. I am getting suspicious of everyone,' Frances shared feeling completely deflated and lost.

Max leaned forward in his chair. 'Then maybe you should leave this to the police,' Frances huffed holding her head in her hands in desperation. 'Come on Frances you've got to believe me.

Frances looked at Max, she felt as though she was staring straight into his soul.

'Surely if I wanted to get rid of her, I would have done it ages ago,' Max tried to reason.

'Where were you the hour before Caroline was found?' Frances questioned him, trying to hide her thoughts from him.

'I was in my classroom,' Max stated.

'Did you see anyone? Can anyone justify where you were?'

'No… I didn't see anybody. But I never left my classroom.'

'Right,' Frances nodded.

'But I didn't do it Frances, whether anyone saw me or not,' Max pleaded.

Frances understood what he was saying. And it was true, anyone could get into that cupboard and a good amount of research could tell you all you needed to know about hydrochloric acid. None of these points truly pointed to Max alone, and Frances knew this. But she was still suspicious of him. Her mind flashed back to the conversation she had with Jonathan:

'You need to be careful because I think someone is trying to frame you for Caroline's death. So be careful with what information you share and with whom.'

Max could easily be framing Frances to save himself or be trying to keep Frances on side to keep himself in the clear by telling her what she wants to hear.

But she also knew that Max isn't the only suspect here, so nobody could be ruled out.

One thing Frances knew for definite is that Jonathan was right, she really couldn't trust anyone anymore.

***

At half past four, Frances had packed everything up and was ready to leave. As she was walking through the school, lugging her heavy bags, she caught a glimpse of the cleaning cupboard. She stood there staring at the door handle, wondering. She made a quick glance around her to see if anyone would see, although she knew she probably didn't need to because there was a high chance, she was the only one still here. Frances shuffled across the hallway and put her bags down by the side of the door, pushed down on the handle and opened the door.

Once inside the cleaning cupboard Frances began her search. It was surprising to think now that this was her first time in here, she hadn't come in here to have a breakdown, and considering the week she'd had that was an achievement. After scanning the bottles, she found what she had been looking for. The bottle labelled hydrochloric acid; three-quarters of the way full. Frances picked up the bottle, she was mesmerised that this bottle had caused so much devastation in such a short amount of time. But then her mind started tickling and she began to wonder:

Why would someone want to do such an awful thing? And more importantly who would want to do such an awful thing?

A Conversation with Kathleen and The Missing Piece...

Tuesday morning couldn't have come quick enough for Frances. She didn't sleep well last night, her mind seemed to be constantly wondering. Even in her sleep she was dreaming about all the possible suspects and their motives. Because of this, Frances wasn't very focused during the school morning either, although she did a very good job of hiding it from everyone; everyone except one.

'You alright Frances? You seem a bit put off today?' Harper queried after letting the children out for lunch.

'Oh yeah I'm alright,' Frances waved Harper off. 'I am just tired. But thank you.'

Harper came and sat next to her. 'You know you don't have to lie to me.'

'Honestly I am fine,' Frances reassured her.

'Look you haven't had the easiest first week here. With Caroline… going, having to handle a lot of this on your own and then to top it off being dragged into the police station for unnecessary questioning! Anyone would understand if you said it was all getting too much,' Harper sympathised.

'I suppose I never thought about all that,' Frances considered. 'But either way, I don't think that's what's worrying me.'

'Then what is it?'

'I just keep thinking about who would do this. And knowing what I know I keep going through the possible suspects and why they would do it, and nothing is making sense,' Frances opened up.

Harper nodded. 'I get that, it is a shame.'

'I just wish I could do more.' Frances sighed.

'I know but we just have to leave it to the police now. I am sure they will have it solved in no time.'

Frances didn't share Harper's optimism, but didn't have time to tell Harper this as all of a sudden, the classroom door swung open, and Dylan stumbled in. 'Hey! PC Plod and his side kick have just pulled up into the car park,' he panted rushing to the window.

'What! Why?' Frances cried as she followed Dylan to the window with Harper hot on her heels.

'How should I know?' Dylan shrieked.

Nearing the end of lunch Frances was in the staffroom making a cup of tea, which she was hoping would clear her head and help her get through the afternoon lessons when Jonathon walked in. He gave her an awkward wave.

'Hello,' she greeted him cheerfully. 'I wasn't expecting to see you here today. For what do we owe the pleasure?'

'Thought we would surprise you,' he joked. 'No, we have come to update Mrs Stevenson on our findings and to gain an understanding on who has access to the chemicals here at the school and what chemicals are contained here.'

'Everyone has access, I could have told you that.'

'Well next time I have a question you'll be my first port of call, although I don't think Chief Inspector Hughes would agree though,' Jonathan chuckled.

'Mm, yeah good point,' she agreed.

'Actually, I'm glad I found you,' Jonathan whispered. 'I have something for you.'

'Oh, a present! You shouldn't have,' Frances gasped clasping her hands together in excitement.

'Ha don't get too excited it's not a present. But it is something you have asked for,' Jonathan chortled. He dug his hands into his pockets and pulled out a piece of folded up paper which he handed to Frances.

'What's this?' She asked, moving the piece of paper between her fingers.

'It's the email address you asked for?' Jonathan murmured.

Frances eyes widened. 'Does the inspector know you have given me this?' She whispered loudly.

Jonathan shook his head placing a finger on his lips, Frances nodded in understanding tapping the side of her nose with her finger. And with that, Jonathan made his way towards the door to find Inspector Hughes. But just before leaving he did turn to Frances nodded at the piece of paper and mouthed something to her and then left:

'Be careful.'

Frances appreciated Jonathan's concern, but she knew that this could be the missing piece of the puzzle. This could give her all the answers. Glancing around the room to check she was alone; Frances slowly peeled the piece of paper open.

To her horror and disappointment, the email address was no clue to her. It didn't give her any answers, the email address gave her all the information she already knew. She was nowhere nearer. She stared at the email address with a heavy heart. All it read was:

HCL@gmail.com

Frances wasn't in a much better place for the rest of the afternoon. Harper kept giving her sympathetic looks, but that was only because she didn't know what Frances knew. She kept trying to tell Harper that she had more news, but she could never find time when Harper was on her own and Harper seemed completely oblivious to Frances' pleading looks. There were so many thoughts going through her head, the email address confirmed what she already knew, that hydrochloric acid was used to kill Caroline. But it gave her no inclination as to who wrote it, that still left her with the list of suspects: Grant, Amanda, Max, even Lennox and Mildred were still in the mix; all with their motives and possible alibis racing through her mind. She was still nowhere nearer.

'Excuse me Miss,' a quiet voice called from behind her. Frances turned around to find the little voice had short brunette hair and youthful piercing blue eyes and was calling for her.

'Hello Kathleen, are you alright? What do you need help with?' Frances greeted the little girl with a friendly smile as she crouched down beside her.

'I'm struggling to see the whiteboard,' Kathleen mumbled, her small delicate hands twisting together nervously. 'I can't read the board when Miss Craig-Lawson uses the blue pen. The teachers always used to use the black board pen.'

'Ah I see,' Frances got thinking. 'How about I get a smaller whiteboard and copy what is on the board onto it. You can have it as your own personal whiteboard to work on?'

Kathleen nodded. 'Thank you, Miss Garnham.'

It was Frances who should be thanking Kathleen really. She appreciated the well needed distraction. So, Frances spent the rest of the afternoon helping little Kathleen as her personal scriber.

Soon enough the end of the school day arrived, and Frances hit a wall of exhaustion. Harper felt the same so made a quick escape home before Frances was able to share the email address, Frances was annoyed at herself for this but knew that the news would keep until tomorrow. She was looking back on the day's events as she started marking the children's work, the marking was split between

Frances and Harper, so Harper had taken her load home with her whilst Frances preferred to keep her work away from home.

As she was sorting the marking into different piles, she came across a piece of work labelled Kathleen's. Her mind instantly went back to the conversation she had had with the little girl that very afternoon:

'Miss Craig-Lawson uses the blue pen. The teachers always used to use the black board pen.'

Frances looked in the pencil pot on the desk and found no black whiteboard pens, so she started searching around the desk for one.

'There must be one in here somewhere,' she muttered racing through the drawers. 'Caroline doesn't seem the type of person to not have prepared a box of pens on standby.' Frances had just reached the bottom drawer of the desk and was losing hope, when she discovered a small box of black lid markers hidden under a pile of paperwork.

'Aha! I knew it, never doubted you Caroline,' she rejoiced as she placed the box onto the desk. 'Better check they still work before I get Harper to use these in her lessons tomorrow. I will look a bit of an idiot if she's trying to write on the board and nothing happens.' She picked up the first black marker pen in the box, turned to face the whiteboard and pulled the lid off the top of the pen.

As she went to press the pen against the whiteboard Frances suddenly came to a halt, something stopped her in her tracks. The smell. It caught her in the back of her throat. She glanced at the blue pen Harper had been using that day, still holding onto the black pen, she pulled the lid off the blue pen and gave it a sniff. It wasn't the same. Something was wrong with this black marker. Just to further prove her point, Frances looked down to find a faint white vapour ascending from the black pen. Something was very wrong. Frances glanced at the other markers in the box and quickly picked another three pens up and took the lids off them.

'Surely they can't all be like this,' Frances pondered. 'This must be a faulty one.' She wasn't confident in this thought, and sure enough white vapour was rising from the three other pens.

Suddenly a thought came into Frances' mind. A distant memory that was triggered by the smell. It felt like déjà vu. Frances was by the door of the classroom, the smell caught in her throat, a chill running down her spine from the open window and all the while her vision was focused on one thing. Caroline's deathly white face against the classroom floor. That was where she recognised the smell from, the day Caroline's body was discovered.

An hour ago, Frances knew nothing, and her head had been full of knotted thoughts, now everything suddenly made sense.

Frances looked at the whiteboard pens and then retrieved the email address out of her pocket, she shook her head in amazement. Another piece of the puzzle clicked into place as Frances raced across the classroom, into the corridor and straight to the whole class picture.

Third row up, eight in from the left.

'Of course,' Frances breathed.

Frances heard the main door opening and the sound of footsteps thundering towards her. Turning her head to the direction of the sound, she was met with the sight of Jonathan haring towards her. 'I'm glad I caught you here,' Jonathan panted. 'Hang on a minute.' Jonathan took a moment to catch his breath before continuing. 'We were trying to find out how Caroline managed to inhale that amount of acid, so we started investigating the evidence we had from the scene of the crime. You'll never guess what we found,' Jonathan exclaimed.

'Did you find hydrochloric acid in the whiteboard pen?' Frances demanded.

Jonathan looked puzzled and slightly put out. 'How did you know that I was going to say that?' He exasperated.

'Long story but I will explain it all to you. But first I need your help, and by yours, I mean both you and Detective Inspector Hughes,' Frances stated as she marched back to the classroom.

'Okay, but… well that sounds serious. What's going on?' Jonathan asked as he chased behind her.

Frances paused in the doorway of the classroom and quickly glanced around to check there was nobody else there. She looked Jonathan in the eye and quietly whispered. 'I know who did this.'

'Wait w-what really?' Jonathan stammered.

'Yes,' she responded flatly.

'But how? I don't understand!'

'Now it's all so clear,' Frances muttered to herself. 'It's so obvious.'

'How is it obvious? Even the inspector is flummoxed by it all!'

'The clues were there, and they have been there all along, we were just too blind to see them. All the comments, the email address. They have been running a mockery of us all.'

'Are you absolutely sure?' Jonathan reiterated as he reached into his jacket pocket for his phone.

'Jonathan I wouldn't joke about something like this,' Frances affirmed.

Jonathan nodded as he dialled a number into his phone and placed the phone to his ear. 'Sir, I'm sorry for calling out of work hours. But you need to come to Arrows Primary Academy. I think you'll want to hear this.' Jonathan immediately hung up and turned his full attention back to Frances. 'So how did you work it out?' Jonathan started, eager to know everything.

'I will reveal all when the chief inspector arrives. But I can tell you one thing,' Frances made her way to the teacher's desk.

'And what's that?' Jonathan queried.

Frances picked up one of the black markers out of the box on the desk and threw it in Jonathan's direction, who caught the pen and gave her a puzzled look.

'The killer has been hiding in plain sight.'

Culprit Confronted and Murderer Unmasked…

'So does everyone know the plan?' Frances asked as she was checking through the slides for the fourth time in the last hour.

'I hope you know what you are doing Miss Garnham? I don't see the point of the presentation or the meeting for that matter,' Barry huffed.

'The presentation and meeting are just diversions so that everyone turns up and doesn't get suspicious. Plus, the presentation has all the evidence on it,' Frances justified. All this negativity from the detective wasn't helping in reassuring Frances in anyway. Jonathan must have sensed this.

'We have officers in the cars outside ready to move on my signal,' Jonathan said with a reassuring smile. Frances nodded in response.

The plan was as follows. The rest of the staff were to arrive in the classroom at four thirty to a meeting planned and given by Frances, but there wasn't a meeting at all. This was the one and only chance to uncover and apprehend the murderer.

The more time went on the more agitated Frances became, she couldn't settle. She kept thinking about everything that could go wrong:

What if she's wrong?

Would she be able to stay here?

Would she then be the main suspect again?

Would she be charged for a murder she did not commit?

But she didn't have time to think about that anymore. The clock struck four thirty, a knock came at the door. The time had come. Frances exchanged a final look with Barry and Jonathan, took a deep breath and got up to open the door.

***

There was a humming murmur as the staff were settling down with their laptops and notebooks. Not that any of them would need them. Frances kept wringing her hands together to distract herself. She glanced around the room, everyone was here. Frances caught Jonathan's eye and gave him a nod to symbolise it was time. He took a long look around the room, taking in each individual person before looking back at Frances and giving her the same nod.

The room fell silent as Frances stood up; all eyes turned on her. 'Umm… hello,' Frances waved. 'Thank you all for coming to this very last-minute meeting.' Frances was rambling, she was dragging this out in fear of the outcome. She took a deep breathe. 'Okay, let's get started. So, this meeting will have one primary focus-'

'Hold on,' a voice spoke out and raised their hand. 'Why are the police here?' Frances traced the hand back to its owner, Ian Marshall.

Before Frances could say anything, a distant voice came to her defence. 'All will become clear soon Sir. Carry on Miss Garnham.'

Frances was startled at the sight of her apparent hero. 'Thank you, Detective Chief Inspector Hughes,' Frances responded and gave him a friendly smile, not that the smile was returned. So, she straightened herself up again and began to fiddle with the laptop, preparing to display the slideshow as she started talking again. 'As I was saying, the meeting will have one primary focus which I hope will put an end to certain... uh how can I say it... sticky situation.'

The staff looked around puzzled. 'What sticky situation would that be?' Grace asked.

Frances took a deep breath and presented the title slide onto the interactive whiteboard for everyone to see. 'This sticky situation.'

The room may have been silent, but Frances didn't need to look at the staff to get an idea of the general consensus from the tension that was now quickly filling the room. The cause of the tension was written in black and white on the slide: *The death of Caroline Macintosh.*' But the silence wouldn't last long.

Adeline stood up; her face was set in a hard stare. 'Frances this is outrageous and completely insensitive. I don't know what kind of joke you think this is, but I find this humour sick and unnerving, and I will not sit here and be witness to it.' Adeline went to walk towards the door, when she was suddenly stopped by a blockage in her path in the form of Jonathan.

'Madam please go back and take your seat,' Jonathan requested.

'You can't make me stay here and listen to this!' Adeline defined.

'Mrs Stevenson please, I am not doing this as some kind of sick joke. I need to share this with you all and put the record straight. Everything will become clear. Please stay,' Frances pleaded with her. She needed to get Adeline onside, otherwise she could have the same issue with everyone else.

'Please take a seat Mrs Stevenson,' Jonathan reiterated gesturing towards her chair.

Adeline glanced at the chair and huffed as she sat down again, shaking her head.

'Thank you,' Frances commented before continuing. 'Caroline's death was both a tragic but mysterious death and I am sure that everyone would agree. However, there was a point in the police's investigation of Caroline's unexpected death where I was their main suspect, I wouldn't be surprised if I still was a suspect to them. But I was taken in for questioning.'

'What! Why? That's ridiculous, you were with us you couldn't possibly have done it!' Dylan cried, looking round to the other staff for clarification to find Alice and Grace nodding in agreement.

'This is what I told them. Which is why I think it's time to clear the air and set the record straight,' Frances announced. She then pressed the space bar on the laptop and the presentation slide changed to a layout of the school. 'I thought to start, I would give a run-down of the whereabouts of everyone the morning of the tragic incident. So myself, Alice, Dylan and Grace were in the staffroom before heading to the hall at about quarter to nine. After speaking to Charlotte, I know that Charlotte was with Adeline and Agatha in the hall. We did briefly see Grant and Ian in the staffroom, so the majority of the staff were in the hall at about five to nine waiting for the meeting to start.'

'Except for Harper who wasn't at the school,' Adeline added giving Harper a supportive tap on her hand. Harper smiled fondly at Adeline.

'Well, that's everyone except Amanda. So where was Amanda that morning?' Grant questioned.

'I was in the office dealing with calls and emails!' Amanda shrieked, looking to Adeline for back up.

Adeline nodded. 'No that's right. Amanda was sorting some errands for me very last minute, which is why I had to quickly call in Charlotte and Agatha to help me.'

'Right, so everyone is accounted for then,' Frances stated to the room.

Everyone agreed. Dylan looked perplexed and then put his hand up to speak. 'So hold on, none of us could have done it then surely?'

Frances nodded. 'You would think that. But what if I told you that nobody had to be in the room for Caroline to have died.'

'That's impossible,' Agatha came back. 'How can someone die if no one is there to kill them?'

'Because Caroline was killed through inhalation of hydrochloric acid that was somewhere in the room.'

'So, we're back at square one again because anyone could have done it,' Alice exasperated.

'No! I don't know how to use hydro- whatever it is,' Amanda defended.

'There are certain people who would know more about the acid so could have easily done it,' Frances announced to the room, looking at Max, Mildred and Lennox as she did so.

'Oh, you can't suggest Mildred and I had anything to do with it surely!' Lennox enraged; he had cottoned on to what Frances was implying.

'Well, you do have knowledge of all the chemicals in the cupboard for when you are cleaning,' Ian inferred.

'Oh Frances! You can't think that you know I would never do anything like that to Caroline. I know we didn't agree on everything but... that would be immoral!' Mildred wailed.

'I know you wouldn't do that Mildred,' Adeline reassured her. 'I mean if we are going with that logic Frances then Max could have done it because he orders the acids in. I'm sorry Max I don't mean to drop you in this,' Adeline stumbled giving Max an apologetic look.

'No need to apologise Adeline. Frances, you know I didn't do it. I wouldn't do something like this,' Max implored.

'Well in all fairness Max, you really did hate Caroline and you saw her the most when having meetings with her,' Dylan reasoned.

'Plus, nobody saw you in the morning before meeting in the hall at five to nine, and your room was next door to hers, so you had ample time,' Charlotte added in agreement.

'Well, it couldn't have been all three of us and I know Mildred and I didn't do it,' Lennox was adamant.

'Come on Frances, I told you if I wanted to get rid of Caroline, I would have done it ages ago. I wouldn't throw away everything I have worked for away just to eliminate Caroline,' Max tried appealing to Frances.

A commotion started to build as staff members were discussing their theories amongst themselves incorporated with the sound of Lennox, Mildred and Max pleading their innocence. Frances tried hushing the noise politely with the help of the two detectives, however seeing as that didn't work Frances had no option but to blow the whistle used for PE lessons has hard as she could. An ear-piercing peep reverberated through the room and stunned the staff to silence. Frances gathered herself together again before speaking to the congregation. 'Before any of you three starts preparing your speech for the jury, I don't think either of you three killed Caroline.'

'Really?' Mildred breathed a sigh of relief.

'Honestly Mildred, I don't think neither you and Lennox or Max did anything to Caroline,' Frances comforted her.

A relieved yet puzzled look fell across their faces. 'Then who did it?' Max queried.

'Well, I'm glad you asked that Max,' Frances began picking up a blue whiteboard pen and went to write something on the board. 'Because the killer has been hiding in plain sight. Let's look again at the weapon used, hydrochloric acid. Now as anyone would know chemicals have a chemical formula, which when you look at the formula for hydrochloric acid you can see that the killer's identity has been there all along.' The staff craned to see the identity as Frances wrote down the chemical formula. Frances turned back to face the culprit. 'Isn't that right, Harper. Craig. Lawson.'

Everyone turned to face Harper. Harper was sat near the back of the room, she looked stupefied.

'What! This… this is ridiculous! Why would I want to kill Caroline? I was just a trainee here!' Harper stuttered. She started hyperventilating looking at Mrs Stevenson with a panicked look. 'Mrs Stevenson I can't do this, why would I- why would I-' Harper gasped between each breathe.

Adeline flew out of her chair quickly followed by Grace, both raced to Harper's side and started comforting her. 'This has gone too far now Frances. First you go around narrowing down my staff making them go against each other and now you are accusing an innocent student of a death she would have no reason to be involved in,' Adeline snapped at Frances.

Grace was still comforting Harper but would occasionally glance at Frances and shake her head at her in disappointment.

'Can I ask you a question Mrs Stevenson? How well do you know Harper?' Jonathan stepped forward.

Adeline looked up to Jonathan and then back at Harper. She continued to do this as she responded. "Um… well… I-I mean not very well no, but I can't imagine that-'

'So perhaps it might be a good idea to listen to Miss Garnham's compelling facts,' Jonathan suggested.

Adeline gave a resigned look and walked back to her seat. 'Very well, but I do think this is a waste of time.'

'Thank you, Inspector Birch,' Frances called to Jonathon. 'There are many facts which correlate Harper to the death of Caroline. Similarly, that Max is an ex-secondary school science teacher and had lots of knowledge about different acids, Harper informed me that she has a science degree at Oxford before she came to train here as a teacher. And as Harper was aware of Max's past profession, she could easily have used the acid and then framed Max for it all.' Frances pointed out. Max gave Harper a suspicious glare before looking back to Frances.

'And because of her extent knowledge, Harper would have known how effective five millilitres of hydrochloric acid would be when it comes to inhalation up close and so would also know the safety precautions to take when using the acid, hence why the windows were closed when I left the classroom, but they were open when I returned with everyone, and we discovered Caroline. But despite her efforts, there was still an unfamiliar smell in the air which made me cough,' Frances continued. She noticed several people consider this and slowly nod as they were remembering their reaction to the pungent smell.

'Is that all you've got?' Harper asked, there was a slight hint of arrogance in her voice.

'The email address,' Frances retorted bluntly. Harper's face dropped ever so slightly. Everybody looked between Harper and Frances confused.

'What email address?' Dylan asked.

'When I was pulled into the station for questioning, the two detectives informed me that they had received an anonymous email telling them about the first interaction I had with Caroline, which didn't end on agreeable terms,' Frances explained. She then turned to face Harper. 'The funny thing is that when we had that discussion there was only one other person in the room. And that was you.'

'Well, isn't that a coincidence,' Harper said with a simple shrug.

'But what made it more ironic was the email address that was used,' Frances ventured further; she pressed the space bar to move the slide on the slideshow. 'At first, we thought the email address was just someone giving us a clue towards what was used to kill Caroline. Because no one would ever be so clued up to use an acid with the chemical formula of their initials, but that was all part of the mind games, wasn't it?'

Harper's response was a smug shrug.

'But one thing I can't understand,' Grace began to ponder. 'How did Harper manage to get the acid into the air, enough to kill Caroline but not hurt anyone else?'

'Well funny you say that, Grace. This flummoxed everyone and was a final piece of the jigsaw, even the police struggled to work it out. It wasn't until I had a conversation with Kathleen that it occurred to me. See Kathleen was struggling to see the blue marker pen on the board, and that's because the teachers always used black pens. So, when I saw a box of black whiteboard pens, I wondered why Harper hadn't used them in her lessons. It wasn't until I opened them then I realised-' Frances went to take the lid off the black pen when she was interrupted.

'Don't!' Harper cried, reaching forward for the pen.

Frances paused for a moment and then vigorously ripped the lid off the pen, soon a familiar pungent smell filled the air and sure enough a white vapour was emitted soon after. Harper rested her head in her hands.

'Harper knew that the pen would be close to Caroline for enough time for her to inhale the acid to kill her, so she dipped the pens into the liquid, filling them up with hydrochloric acid. But you couldn't risk doing one pen in case she didn't pick that pen, so you did a whole new box full just in case. That's why you used the blue pen yesterday instead of black, and you'd thought no one had noticed. But little Kathleen did, without even realising it.'

The room went quiet, realisation was setting in.

'Oh Harper,' Agatha sighed regretfully. 'Why would you do such a thing?'

'Perhaps this will answer your question Agatha,' Frances skipped onto the next slide on her presentation and there was the old whole school photo again. Harper looked at the photo and shuffled uncomfortably in her seat. The other staff looked fondly at the picture which then became perplexed as they began to wonder at the significance behind the photograph. 'Mildred, would you be able to look at the photo again please, specifically third row up eighth child in from the left. Who does it remind you of?' Frances asked, looking at an uncomfortable Harper. 'Look at how young you looked back then.'

Mildred peered at the photo for a minute and then followed Frances' gaze unsure of what she was meant to be looking at. And then it dawned on her. 'You! Of course, I knew I recognised the child, it was you!' Mildred gasped, pointing at Harper.

'What was it you said to me Harper? *You didn't like how Caroline spoke to the children. It reminded you of how you were treated when you were at school,*' Frances pointed at the child in the photo. 'Because that's how Caroline treated you wasn't it? And now you wanted revenge-'

'Caroline was a bitch. So up herself, thought she could never do wrong,' Harper interrupted bitterly.

Frances paused, dumbfound by Harper's response. 'She hadn't changed a bit, had she?' She responded quietly.

'She was so blind sighted by her own self-worth, she didn't recognise me after all these years,' Harper muttered before continuing in a cynical tone. 'But I had the last laugh when I was able to give her her very own reunion as she struggled to catch her breathe. I wasn't sure what scared her more, being reminded of her wretched past or watching her sad little life flash before her eyes and her not having a single way of stopping it.'

Mildred looked at her horrified. 'You're a monster,' she whispered.

'I'm not a monster she was!' Harper snapped back, raising her voice. 'She was vile, evil. She didn't deserve to teach. I don't deserve any of this!'

'Neither did Caroline!' Frances snapped.

Once again, the room was silent, but the tension was so loud.

Barry tried to move the discussion on, sensing that if the argument carried on things could turn nasty. 'But Harper told us that she arrived at the school at five to nine. So how could she have done all of that in that short amount of time?' He challenged.

Harper laughed. 'Call yourself a detective? You naive little man,' she sneered. 'Caroline was practically through death's door when I finally arrived. All I had to do was check my work was enough and had done the damage, so I then opened the windows before rushing into the hall playing the role of the traumatised student. And you all bought it... I should have been an actress,' Harper seemed proud of all the damage she had caused, Frances couldn't bare to look at her anymore. But she wasn't done with her yet.

'And the anonymous email you sent to police about me?' Frances interrogated.

Harper shrugged. 'What can I say, you were an ideal target. Although I did feel bad for you... pity really. We could have been a good team you and I, especially when I realised that you could have Caroline's job. That's when my thoughts turned to who else could be an easy target. So, I turned to those who also know a lot about the side effects of the different chemicals,' Harper turned to face Lennox, Mildred and Max. 'It's just a shame you remembered all about my past training; I might have gotten away with it then.'

'That's why you framed Max because you knew he would be the obvious person, but you were the one who asked him about the side effects. Was that your research for murdering Caroline?' Frances snapped.

'Ding ding ding! We have a winner!' Harper shouted, pointing to Frances, looking completely unfazed by the whole situation.

Frances was dumbfounded. Not only was Harper openly admitting to the murder to Caroline

Macintosh, but she was also now saying that she was going to frame Frances for the murder until she realised that she could use Frances to her advantage. This infuriated her, she wanted to wipe the smirk off Harper's face, but she wouldn't sink to that level. So instead, Frances would get at Harper the only way she knew how. 'I suppose you want me to feel honoured that you saved me then,' Frances retaliated sarcastically.

Harper's response started off with a shrug. 'No need to thank me. I was just doing my job, helping people out,' She responded simply.

Frances started to slowly walk across the room towards Harper, at this point Barry and Jonathan had already started to creep towards Harper. This was her moment. 'You said to me that as part of your job you wanted to make sure other children weren't given the same experience you had at school,' Frances started casually, edging closer and closer towards Harper.

Harper nodded, a sly smirk forming across her face.

Frances leant across the desk, her face closing into Harper's. 'Well, I would like to see how you are going to do that behind prison bars,' she spat at Harper.

Harper's face dropped, she glanced either side of her to discover Jonathan and Barry there, trapping her.

Barry decided enough was enough and took control. 'Harper Craig-Lawson, I am arresting you for the murder of Miss Caroline Macintosh...' As Barry continued to talk, his voice became a blur in the background of Frances' mind. Her ears were ringing, the image of Harper's smug face was constantly replaying in her mind. She was becoming frantic, she was seething with anger, her heart was racing, but she couldn't snap out of it. After several slow deep breathes and squeezing her fists tightly shut, Barry's voice slowly became louder again, drowning out the parading thoughts terrorising her mind. 'You do not have to say anything, but it may harm your defence if you do not mention when questioned something which you later rely on in court, and anything you do say may be given in evidence.'

The click of the handcuffs being closed made Frances turn to see Harper being escorted out of the classroom. She walked to the window and watched as Harper left the reception main doors and strolled across the car park before slowly clambering into the back of the police car. The slam of the car door meant one thing to Frances. Justice.

Dust Settles and Foes Forgiven...

Frances was shielding her eyes from the setting sun as she watched the police car roll out of the car park and into the still village of Bertley. Jonathan came and stood beside her in the silence, it was only after the car had disappeared from view that Jonathan spoke. It was as though they feared Harper would still be able to hear them if they spoke.

'Well, I have to say you definitely know how to present your case to an audience, especially for a novice detective,' Jonathan chuckled expecting Frances to join in. But instead, Frances stayed silent, Jonathan turned to her with a look of concern. 'Frances are you okay?' He asked.

'I just don't understand,' Frances mumbled quietly, 'Harper had so much of the future ahead of her. She was a bright girl; she would have gone far in life. Why throw it all away like this?'

Jonathan sighed. 'Sometimes revenge takes over,' He explained with a shrug.

'I suppose you're right,' Frances paused for a moment and then shook off those thoughts and turned to Jonathan. 'Anyway, thank you for all your help and basically giving me the answers,' Frances laughed.

'Anytime,' Jonathan laughed. 'But I really think I should be thanking you for solving the case.'

Frances thought about it and nodded in agreement, the two laughed out loud, although the laughter soon stopped as Detective Barry Hughes strolled purposefully into the room, making a bee line for the pair.

'Right, Harper is on her way to the police station and will be charged when she arrives there and I have just received feedback from my officers, they have arrived at her student accommodation and have found a small bottle with traces of hydrochloric acid within it. It has been taken to the lab to test for her fingerprints,' Barry stated. Jonathan and Frances nodded. 'Um, I want to thank you for helping... actually solving the case,' Barry awkwardly turned to Frances. 'I don't think we started on the right foot, so I apologise for my behaviour. I was extremely rude and underestimated your points of view, I realise now you are more than capable of... anyway I'm sorry Miss Garnham,' Barry fumbled awkwardly.

Frances was amazed by Barry's apology. She wasn't expecting anything like that from him, at the end of the day she interfered when she shouldn't have so he had every right to be annoyed with her. But now she understood Jonathan's point, Barry Hughes can be a different person when you get to know him. 'There's no need to apologise,' Frances waved a hand at Barry as she shook her head. 'However, maybe now could drop the Miss Garnham?'

Barry looked startled at the response, but then nodded and chortled. Jonathan joined in and laughed but caught Barry looking at him with a stern expression and immediately stopped. 'But what I did wonder was exactly how Frances managed to obtain certain knowledge related to the case which was strictly confidential,' Barry raised an eyebrow at Jonathan. 'Would you care to explain yourself Detective Birch?'

Jonathan stuttered and stammered, fiddling with his tie as he tried to find a believable explanation for

Detective Hughes; luckily Frances jumped in to save him.

'Please don't blame Detective Birch, I practically cornered him at one point in order to drag information out of him, so if anyone needs to be blamed it's me.'

'Well in that case, we will speak no more about it. Right, I must be going. I will need to make myself available for questioning when the update is announced to the general public,' Barry turned to Frances. 'I wish you all the best Miss- Frances. I hope that if we do ever meet again, it will not be in a similar situation.'

'Yes, I hope so too. Goodbye Detective Hughes,' Frances responded fondly.

Barry turned to leave, as he did so he faced Jonathan and leaned towards him. 'You are very lucky this time that someone is willing to take the blame for you. I will be watching you in the future though,' Barry gave Jonathan a threatening look before walking away in order to hide the small smirk forming on his face.

Jonathan turned to Frances puffing out a deep breathe, he chuckled and mouthed 'Thank you,' to Frances who gave a shrug and grinned. 'A good thing out of all this though, it looks like you finally managed to win Barry Hughes round!' Jonathan nudged Frances sounding impressed.

'I know who would have thought it! It did take me a while though,' Frances giggled.

As though he could hear them, Barry suddenly called for Jonathan from another room telling him that they needed to get going to the station.

'Coming Sir,' Jonathan called back, he then turned back to Frances. 'Well looks like that's my cue. I best get going.'

Frances nodded. 'Yeah, well thank you again for everything. Especially putting your job on the line to share police findings with me.'

'Hey no worries. Anytime, as long as the next time I ever need help on a case-' Jonathan started.

'Give me a call and I'll be there!' Frances finished.

And with a final shared laugh, Jonathan collected his things and left the classroom making his way to join Barry Hughes outside.

* * *

'Ah Frances, I am glad I caught you on your own,' Adeline approached Frances as she was closing down her slideshow. 'I wanted to come and apologise for my behaviour during the meeting. It was completely unprofessional of me.'

'Honestly Adeline there is no need for you to apologise,' Frances soothed. 'I am sure anyone else would have reacted the same if someone was accusing their staff members of murder.'

'I just can't get my head around how Harper could do such an awful thing,' Adeline rubbed her temples. Frances nodded, she couldn't think of any response, so the pair fell into silence.

Adeline was the first to speak. 'Frances this may be very cheeky of me, but how would you feel about becoming the year one teacher? Even if it's just temporarily until I can find a replacement.'

Frances considered it. She had decided to steer clear of teaching roles, but surely she would be stupid to turn this down? And would Adeline keep her on if she didn't? When reflecting on the turn of events since she joined this school, surely taking on a class of thirty wouldn't be the toughest challenge she has faced? 'Yeah, that's absolutely fine, until a new teacher is found of course,' Frances accepted as confidently as she could muster.

'That's fantastic, thank you! Yes, I will get onto that… first thing in the morning,' Adeline clapped her hands together, giving Frances a grin and practically skipped out of the classroom.

After a short while the other members of staff slowly dwindled out into their own classrooms and headed straight home.

'Are you sure you should be a teacher and not a detective?'

Frances jumped round to find Dylan, Agatha and Grace sat there. She had assumed everyone had gone home, but now clearly, she was wrong. 'I'm positive! I think that was just a fluke,' Frances chuckled. 'And anyway, it wasn't just me, I must thank Kathleen for her unknown help in solving the case. If we hadn't of spoken that afternoon, I would have still been none the wiser!'

Dylan shrugged. 'I still think you're in the wrong job.' Frances rolled her eyes.

Grace came to save Frances from the awkward conversation. 'Are you trying to get rid of Frances Dylan?' She demanded as she playfully hit him on the arm.

'Frances can't leave anyway,' Agatha chipped in as she shut the lip of her laptop closed. 'We don't have anyone else to take over the year one class.'

The two women laughed as everyone went to leave the classroom, they turned to check that Frances was following and found her in the middle of the room frozen to the spot with a concerned look on her face.

'Frances whatever is the matter dear?' Grace asked concerned.

'It's just dawned on me, I have drawn the short straw,' Frances announced throwing her hands up in despair. 'I have to take on a class of thirty children... and the only help I had I've just sent to prison!'

The End.

Acknowledgements

Well, where to start! It's safe to say my life has completely changed, my career path along has done a 360 spin! So, my message to those who don't know what they want to do in life or have an idea and are scared it won't work out, this is your sign! You only live once, so why waste life wondering about the what ifs? You don't know until you try!

I would first like to thank my family (those who knew about the book that is!) for the support along the way. Mainly my dad Barry, Ian and Darren (Hatter). Also, a big surprise and thanks to my friends and family for the name inspirations for some of the characters!

Thank you to my Aunt June (Mildred - in memory of Karen) for reading my book and giving me your opinions.

To my best furiend Bertie. Thank you for keeping me company with snuggles for many hours as I was tapping away on the laptop or scribbling notes. I'm sorry if I ever disturbed your precious nap times.

You are the best furry friend a girl could ask for. If you haven't already guessed Bertley was named in your honour. I love you lots little man xxx

And finally, to my mum Kathy. My unhinged bracket. Thank you for the encouragement and support with writing this book. Thank you for being my first editor and reading the first EVER draft of this book, you will be the only person to ever see my atrocious spelling mistakes and my laptop's idea of autocorrecting! Thank you for telling me to keep going and to ignore the doubt, but mostly thank you for keeping this book a secret for so long! I genuinely don't think I can find enough words to truly thank you, but I am going to give it a go. Thank you for being a constant cheerleader throughout my life, from the beginning in nursery and primary school all the way through secondary school and college and finally helping me through the trails, tribulations and tears through university - big emphasis on the tears! Thank you for picking me up when I was down and pushing me to carry on when I didn't think I was good enough. Thank you for all the laughter and tears (most of those tears being tears of laughter) and thank you for all the amazing times we have had together, both the big and small memories we will make together. Thank you for all you have done for our family - especially for me because I know I can be a pain! I feel like you don't hear this enough, but I am so proud of you, for all you have done and achieved and all the struggles and obstacles you have had to overcome. I can say hand on heart that this book wouldn't have happened, and I wouldn't be the person I am today without you.

Thank you for being my best friend and my mum. I love you xxx

About The Author

Hannah Jones, born 24th April 2000 and living in Lincoln, recently graduated with her teaching degree. The four years' experience of writing essays will come in handy as she turns her focus to writing. Her knowledge of teaching makes for the perfect theme for her first murder mystery novel, which she is hoping to make into a series.

Hannah's first novel is Academy Assassination.

Printed in Great Britain
by Amazon